"Words aren't enough, Esther," Dan said fiercely, pulling her into her room and closing the door behind him.

"I can't explain the way you fill me so completely. My mind, my body, my soul . . . or whatever it is that keeps me alive, keeps me looking forward to living from one moment to the next—everything is focused on you. I have this insane, almost animal-like need to possess you, to take care of you and protect you. I—I'm actually crazy in love with you," he finished.

Esther had the strange sensation she was falling apart at the seams. The passion and power in Dan was numbing, even though her heart was racing wildly and something in her was screaming for fewer words and more action. "Show me," she whispered raggedly. "Now."

Into Dan's eyes came the wild, desperate need he'd tried to describe, and Esther felt fear and excitement all at once. She nearly screamed when his hands reached out for her. But they were the gently deft and experienced hands of a man who loved her, of a man who knew what he wanted. It was what she wanted too. . . .

WHAT ARE *LOVESWEPT* ROMANCES?

They are stories of true romance and touching emotion. We believe those two very important ingredients are constants in our highly sensual and very believable stories in the *LOVESWEPT* line. Our goal is to give you, the reader, stories of consistently high quality that may sometimes make you laugh, sometimes make you cry, but are always fresh and creative and contain many delightful surprises within their pages.

Most romance fans read an enormous number of books. Those they truly love, they keep. Others may be traded with friends and soon forgotten. We hope that each *LOVESWEPT* romance will be a treasure—a "keeper." We will always try to publish

LOVE STORIES YOU'LL NEVER FORGET
BY AUTHORS YOU'LL ALWAYS REMEMBER

The Editors

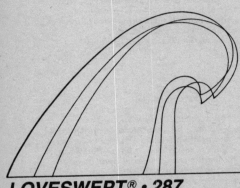

LOVESWEPT® • 287

Mary Kay McComas
Obsession

BANTAM BOOKS
TORONTO • NEW YORK • LONDON • SYDNEY • AUCKLAND

OBSESSION

A Bantam Book / October 1988

LOVESWEPT® and the wave device are registered
trademarks of Bantam Books, a division of
Bantam Doubleday Dell Publishing Group, Inc.
Registered in U.S. Patent
and Trademark Office and elsewhere.

If you would be interested in receiving protective vinyl
covers for your Loveswept books, please write to this address
for information:

Loveswept
Bantam Books
P.O. Box 985
Hicksville, NY 11802

ISBN 0-553-21939-1

Published simultaneously in the United States and Canada

*This book is for
all the dedicated dreamers
I know and love. You are
truly the intrepid ones.*

Prologue

Excerpts from a young girl's diary:

"Mama says I should consider myself lucky and be grateful for all I've got. I guess that depends on which side of the fence you're looking over."

"I don't think I'm so lucky not to know who my father is, but I'm grateful to be alive.

"I don't think I'm so lucky to be the 'Bastard of Bellewood,' but I'll be grateful to leave someday.

"I don't think I'm so lucky because I can't go on to school next year like Jewel Avery, but I'm grateful that I'm smart and strong enough to go after what I want anyway. I will make it someday.

"I don't think I'm so lucky because I can't sing worth beans, but I'm grateful for Addy Markham's piano and for all the words I know. Such good words that comfort me when I'm hurt or lonely. Beautiful sounds and phrases that clutter my mind when I'm happy, feeling free, or excited.

"I don't think I'm so lucky like Mama says, but I'm grateful things aren't any worse.

"Addy Markham says I'm a dreamer and that it's too

bad, because dreamers lead painful lives. I tried to tell her my life isn't always going to be the way it is now. I told her I was going to be rich and famous and loved someday, but she only laughed.

"The river flooded again the day before yesterday. Folks say it's never gotten this high before, but all I know is that after it does flood, the mess and destruction are incredible. Why the company chose to build so close to the river is beyond me.

"Anyway, Mama offered to put the Averys up until they could make better arrangements. But they told Mama they didn't think it would be good for Jewel— who was still too young and innocent to understand—to be exposed to "the misbegotten circumstances associated with you." I assumed they meant me. They hurt Mama's feelings, but I just laughed. If they knew how innocent Jewel *really* was, they'd probably wet their pants. Mrs. Fischer and her children came to stay instead, and I'm having lots of fun playing with the babies. . . .

"I was on my way home. Tommy followed me. He kissed me on my mouth, bit my neck, and tore my shirt. I threw dirt in his face and bit his wrist as hard as I could. He told me I was like my mama, that I'd come begging when Mama lost her job, and he'd take me then. I'd rather die.

"They killed Charity Keyser's dog today. Tommy Belldon said it bit him, so they shot it in the head, and poor old Charity cried.

"I hate Bellewood and every sorry soul in it. After I told Mama what Tommy did, my long-lost father finally made an appearance. He, too, is gifted with sweet words, but after all this time they don't mean much.

"I can't stay any longer and I won't ever be back. Mama will be better off without me. Then again, she may not even notice I'm gone. Her grief is great for the man who fathered me. His wife gave me one thousand dollars to get out of town, and in return she said she would see to it that no harm came to my mother, and as long as I stay away, Mama will be well cared for. With my father gone and my mother nearly mindless in her grief, the secret of my birth is that it never really happened anyway. It's as if I don't really exist anymore. But I do. I do to me. I'm alive. I'm Esther Brite and I'm sixteen years old. And there isn't anything I can't do once I set my mind to it."

One

They were watching her. She could feel them staring at her. She didn't care, she'd been stared at before, lots of times. Clamorous hordes of people had jostled one another just to catch a glimpse of her. Still, this was no ordinary gathering, and she wasn't at her very best these days.

Why had she come, she wondered. At the time it had seemed imperative; now she wasn't so sure. And why would she come in February? Lord, it was cold here. How could she have forgotten the dreary gray winter skies, the bare, lifeless trees, the bitter wind. Maybe a moribund place like this suited her state of mind.

Elephants had a special dying place, so did salmon and whales, she remembered. She was weak and tired. Her vision was blurred and her bones ached. Maybe she'd come home to die. . . .

He stood among the townspeople and watched her walk slowly across the street from the drugstore toward the flashy little red sports car that could only have belonged to her.

Tall, too thin and pale, she held her head self-consciously high. Her long dark hair whipped about her face in the harsh winds, but she didn't move to restrain it. It was as if she didn't realize how cold and windy it was. All she wore was a bulky knit sweater and a pair of well-worn jeans that hugged her long, slim legs closely. The black leather boots she wore were probably very fashionable somewhere else, he decided, but they were totally inadequate here.

He watched as she stumbled on the slick asphalt once, then again, before she was close enough to get a grip on her car and hold herself up. She raised her face to the wind, then got into the car. His eyes narrowed as he saw her head back fall back on the headrest. His heart counted the seconds until she would start the car and drive back to the motel. Then his pulse rate quickened, telling him something was wrong.

Esther gulped the frigid air. She closed her eyes against the dimness that was consuming her. Was this what dying felt like, she wondered. Her thoughts, memories, and emotions raced as reality began to slip away from her.

"Ms. Brite," a stern voice called out from the darkness. "Esther. Esther, wake up," a man shouted, and she felt a stinging force on her cheek. "Dammit, Esther, don't do this. Esther!"

The man who owned the deep, gruff voice was rude and mean. How dare he shake her as if she were a cheap rag doll. Didn't he know who she was?

"Dammit, Esther, wake up." His tone was fierce.

"Get your damned hands off me," she muttered, too weak even to open her eyes.

"When you wake up, I'll let go," he said, patting her face sharply and repeatedly.

Esther swore at him, wanted to punch him, but couldn't.

"Thatta girl. Show a little spunk," he said in an encouraging tone.

She groaned. "Spunk. Hell."

"Are you on drugs?" he asked firmly.

Esther swore at him again.

"Good. Have you been sick long? You're burning with fever," he told her, sounding angry and disapproving.

"Fever?" She only had tried to think of the word, but she'd said it aloud.

"That's right, fancy pants," he said in a calmer but not much nicer tone as he started to scoop her up and out of the car.

"No. Don't. Leave me alone," she protested, not sure of what was happening, desperately trying to become fully alert and protect herself.

About the time her eyes finally opened, she was being placed quickly and yet rather gently into the passenger's side of her car. The door slammed closed and a big, dark-haired man got in beside her on the driver's side.

"Keys," he ordered, holding out a large hand with long slim fingers and turning dark, intense brown eyes on her.

"Who the hell are you?" she asked.

His eyes, so deep and consuming, were like two endless vacuums pulling at her disjointed senses.

"My name is Dr. Daniel Jacobey," he told her clearly. "You're ill. You need help."

"Doc Evans isn't dead, is he?" she asked, trying to recall the event, making an exerted effort to resist the lure of the man's eyes.

"Retired," he stated, wiggling his fingers at her impatiently.

"Oh" was her only comment as she patted various parts of her body, then slipped her fingers into the pocket of her sweater to retrieve the car keys. She flipped them into the doctor's hand and leaned back into the seat with a tired sigh, closing her eyes fatalistically. Whatever happened now would happen. Lethargy was setting in again, and she'd depleted enough of her energy by asking who the man was. She'd have to trust him.

She must have begun dreaming soon after that, as people and faces floated in and out of her consciousness like shadows from the past . . . except the doctor was in them too.

His hands were cool and gentle. He spoke softly to her and touched her cheek with great tenderness. Addy Markham came to chide her, but she'd always spoken harshly without meaning to. It was just her way. She was older now, which seemed odd. Esther could hear her mother's voice from far away but never saw her face. She even dreamed that the townspeople were gathering to shoot her in the head for biting Tommy Belldon. She had to leave town. She had to get away before they all found out the truth about her. Esther ran. She ran hard. Hands grabbed her, held her. They were cool and gentle and soothing. They were nice hands and she gave herself up to them, feeling safe and content.

"Feeling better?"

Esther heard the question but hoped if she ignored it, whoever wanted to know would go away.

"People say you're a genius, but if you ask me, you're pretty stupid. No genius would let herself get this sick."

It was that idiot doctor again.

"Who asked you?" Esther mumbled into her pillow.

"No one," Dan replied. "But if someone had, that's what I'd tell them."

Esther opened one eye and glared at him. "What is your name again?"

"Dan Jacobey."

"Am I still in Bellewood?"

"Yes."

"That figures. Your bedside manner and Bellewood were made for each other. It's probably the only town in the world that'd take you and be happy to have you," she said sarcastically. Besides, she added to herself, what kind of doctor would wear soft worn blue jeans and thick flannel shirts during office hours? She was very careful, however, not to admit to herself how virile and rugged he looked in them.

"Now, don't you go bad-mouthin' Doctor Dan, Esther Brite. Ya owe him your life, and that ain't no way to pay him back." Addy Markham spoke sharply from the doorway, then entered the room with a tray of food.

Esther's face was a grimace of misery as she tried to lift her head off the pillow and focus her eyes on Addy. The action required too much effort, and she let her face fall into the pillow and groaned defeatedly. Not only was she as weak as a kitten, but she appeared to be at the mercy of the charming Dr. Delightful *and* Addy Markham.

"Addy's right," the doctor agreed, throwing back the sheets that covered Esther. He helped her sit up in bed, saying, "And I always demand full restitution for my services."

"Do you take out-of-town checks?" Esther quipped as she allowed him to prop pillows behind her.

"No. And I don't accept American Express either," he was anticipating her.

She slid Dan a glance, her exotic, almond-shaped green eyes suspicious. "That leaves barter, Doctor. Are you planning on taking your payment out in trade?" she asked, not threatened or afraid, merely curious.

His eyes warmed with amusement, and for a brief moment Esther took a keen and special liking to the doctor. Without the cool manner, he was very appealing.

"Yes," he replied, a cunning half smile on his lips. "I'll trade my skills and the saving of your life for a little cooperation."

Esther's brows rose, her eyes unflinchingly clear as she met his gaze.

"You're rundown, malnourished, and you nearly died of pneumonia. Your payment is to get yourself well and strong." His expression was serious again. "I want you to cooperate with Addy. Eat when she tells you, rest when she says to. Take your pills and stay in bed."

Esther was thoughtful as she took in her surroundings for the first time. Her response to his conditions faded as she noticed there was something familiar about the room. She knew she wasn't at Addy's house. The shape and size of the room and the view from the window were very familiar, but the cracking plaster walls she remembered had been covered with cedar paneling, and . . . a rug covered the floor, wall to wall.

"This is my house," she said in amazement, feeling dazed and weak again. Maybe she was still dreaming.

"No. It's my house," the doctor said, following her gaze around the room, trying to see things from her perspective, aware that she must have left many memories in this room. Was she seeing paneling or peeling plaster?

"My mother's house," she said. "My old room. So long ago . . ."

Her memories and emotions were abruptly disturbed by Addy firmly placing the tray on her lap.

"Doctor Dan did a fine job fixin' it up. Next to the Big House, it's probably the nicest in town now, so don't you go spoiling it for him," Addy scolded as she handed a spoon to Esther and removed the cloth covering the tray to reveal a bowl of dark broth, another of red gelatin, and a cup of sweet-smelling tea.

Esther ran a hand through her long, tangled hair and glanced from Addy to the doctor.

"I wouldn't want to spoil it for him. It looks great," she said, feeling ill-at-ease for the first time in a long time. "Mama always wanted to fix it up nice," she told the doctor, then looked to Addy. "I don't know why she . . ." Esther trailed off, dropping her gaze regretfully.

"Ms. Brite will probably have a hard time eating for a while. Would you help her, Addy? I have patients to see. Call me if you need me," the doctor said brusquely. He hadn't reached the door before Esther began to cough, and Addy hastily retrieved the tray.

It was a hard cough, causing Esther to wheeze and gasp for air, nearly choking her as she bent over to get her breath back.

"Relax and try to breathe deeply," he said. Esther tried but only succeeded in initiating a whole new episode of coughing.

Dan held her upper arm and placed a comforting hand on her back while she fought to breathe. Oddly, her body seemed conditioned to the touch of his hands. She sensed he could be trusted to care for her, to protect her. Even as she gasped for air, she didn't doubt she was safe.

"Those are bronchospasms. You'll have them until your lungs clear up. The medication will help," he told her as she began to relax once again.

Esther thought he was a little cold. Doc Evans had been a much more compassionate man. She wished he were there instead of this hard, matter-of-fact man with his perceptive hands and alluring eyes.

"Eat up. I'll be back later," he said.

The two women watched him exit, their opinions of him on opposite ends of the spectrum.

"Good man," commented Addy.

Esther shrugged. "It's hard to tell from what I've seen."

"Well, he sat up with you for three nights until your fever broke and you fought your way back to life. I coulda done it, but he said he wanted to. He said nights were usually the worst, and he wanted to be close in case somethin' happened," Addy said, then reiterated, "He's a good man."

"I'll take your word for it," Esther said, too tired to fight but still wanting to talk to Addy.

"I've been here three days?" she asked feebly.

"Can't say where you were in your head," the old woman said, "but your body's been here that long. He coulda kept you at his little clinic, but he took you into his home. He offered to pay me for carin' for ya, but I told him I cared for ya when you was little, I cared for your ma after that, and I could do for you again without gettin' paid for it."

A slow smile of remembrance came to Esther's lips as she looked at Addy Markham, really seeing her for the first time in many years.

As a young woman, Addy had owned the local brothel in the one-horse, one-whore town of Bellewood. Later, she'd taken on three, sometimes four assistants. Esther's mother had been among them for a short time, before Laura had gotten a better job in the offices at Belldon Mines.

Given her mother's tainted history and the fact that she'd borne a bastard child, Esther realized that one of the few people in town who'd had a friendly word for Laura Brite was her old employer, Addy Markham.

Addy Markham was gruff, straightforward, and to-the-point. There was a certain grace about Addy's tall, thin stature. She'd dressed simply but expensively in tailored clothes. She'd worn her dark hair long and wound into a tight knot at the top of her head, and yet she was always careful to allow a few soft, curling tendrils to escape. She never was the picture-book image of a madam.

Not much about the woman had changed over the years except that her hair was completely gray and she looked a little tired to Esther who'd known her as a younger woman. She'd aged well, however, Esther admitted as she took in the woman's smooth skin. Her face was carefully made up to enhance her blue eyes, thin straight nose, and lips that had seduced more than their fair share of men.

"Thanks, Addy," Esther said quietly, meaning it as much for now as for times in the past. "You look well."

"A lot you care," she said, replacing the tray in Esther's lap, then sitting on the bed, picking up the spoon. "I ain't heard from ya since your mama died. I only heard then because you wanted to make sure she was buried properly"

Esther couldn't speak. There was nothing to say. Seventeen years ago she'd left Bellewood, her mother, and Addy Markham behind her to make a new life for herself. Addy knew why she'd left and how she'd felt at the time. She knew and she understood. There was nothing more for either one to say. So why did Esther feel guilty all of a sudden?

Addy had always known how to reach her if necessary, and Esther had always remembered Addy at Christmas and on her birthday. Of course, she hadn't been informed until months later that Addy had had her gallbladder removed in an emergency operation. She was completely recovered by the time Esther found out. Esther might have come back to Bellewood if Addy had asked or had needed her, but she'd never given any indication that she desired to see her. Come to think of it, Addy had never asked for anything from Esther—not an autographed album, not a loan, not even the time of day. She'd simply been there. Good ol' Addy, Esther thought.

Esther had to admit that she could have made more of an effort to keep in touch with Addy over the years. Addy probably would have appreciated it more than her own mother had, and she'd owed it to Addy who had been the only friend she'd known in those early years. She had been more of a mother to Esther than Laura Brite had ever been.

Addy fed Esther the broth and gelatin silently for a

while, and then spoke as if the conversation hadn't lapsed.

"He was real good to her too," she commented. "He'd listen to her ramble on the way she did toward the end."

"The doctor?" Esther clarified, knowing Addy was thinking of Laura.

Addy nodded. "He came here about five years ago, just before your mama died. I think maybe he had some problems of his own when he came, but we were glad to have him once we got to know him. He was some sort of highfalutin' doctor from D.C.; he came as a favor to Doc Evans, who's a friend of his uncle's. It was only supposed to be temporary-like, till they could find a replacement, but he's been here ever since," she reported to Esther, indicating the man was due his proper respect. "Anyway," she continued, offering Esther some tea, "your mama took a shine to him when she was in her right mind, and he was real kind to her. He even went to her funeral, and he hadn't known her long."

"Is that why he's being so rough on me? Because he, a virtual stranger, went to her funeral, and her own daughter didn't show up?" Esther asked.

"I don't think so," Addy said, considering, as she rose and took the tray away. "I don't know why he's testy with you, but it don't matter anyway. You ain't goin' to be here forever." She paused briefly, then bluntly asked, "Why did you come back here, Esther?"

"I don't know," she said, shaking her head limply. "It may have been fever-induced, but I remember thinking there was an answer here for me. A solution to a lot of things I've been thinking about lately."

"Don't know what it could be," the old woman said. "All the answers you got to the questions ya asked as a girl weren't ones ya wanted to hear. And except for the doctor, things ain't changed much."

"Well, I'll hang around for a couple of days and give folks something to talk about, and then I'll leave," Esther said lightly, wishing she *could* remember the half-baked idea that had sent her speeding from New York to this godforsaken place in the hills of West Virginia.

She watched Addy Markham preparing to leave her. She took the capsules the woman gave her and swallowed them down with cool water. Without further words, Addy moved to the door, the tray in her hands. She hesitated, then turned to face Esther once again. Her face took on a sorrowful, sincere look that the younger woman had seen only once before, and finally she spoke with great difficulty. "I . . . I wept sorely for your losses, Esther. To lose a man you love is a terrible, painful thing. To lose his baby, your child . . . well, there ain't no greater pain. Of all the misfortunes in your life, I wish you coulda been spared that one."

Esther nodded in appreciation, for the unexpected empathy Addy had shown, then closed her eyes to ward off the tears that threatened to spill. When she opened them again, Addy was gone.

She took the time to make a closer inspection of her old room, unable to prevent all the memories that came rushing back to her. This was quite a room, she thought. Here the infamous Esther Brite had cried, been lonely, raged with anger. Here she'd steeled herself the night she'd left it for good seventeen years before, steeled herself to succeed and to leave all of what she could call her security—if she really stretched the word.

Esther's gaze fell to the floor and the thick rust-colored carpet covering it. She considered how warm it must be on cold winter mornings, compared to the frigid wooden planks beneath it. She ran a toe along the scar on the bottom of her right foot, recalling the day she'd cut a deep gash there on a raised nail in a loose plank. She wondered if that plank was still loose as she drifted off to sleep.

Two

Dan Jacobey released a deep sigh of hopeless frustration as he leaned against the doorjamb of Esther's bedroom watching her sleep. Lord, she was beautiful, he thought again for the umteenth time. He never dreamed he'd get this close to her, let alone lay his hands on her body. It was more like a nightmare, actually. He felt like a pubescent boy every time he entered the same room she was in. His heart raced, his body quickened, his tongue tied itself in knots.

He had been terrified that she was dying when he'd first seen her in the car. His fear expressed itself in anger, and she had responded to it. Dan found it easier and safer to keep up the gruff, angry pretense to hide his true feelings for her. Men probably fell all over themselves to impress her. He just couldn't let her see how much she'd come to mean to him.

He couldn't place the exact time or day his one-sided romance with Esther Brite had begun. It had come to him slowly, in stages, creating a disconcerting paradox that he toiled with frequently. It was like the plot of an old gothic movie, where the hero falls in love with a portrait of a beautiful young woman who's been dead for several centuries. It had been that unreal for him at first, but later it had taken on a life of its own, had become real and uncontainable.

The whole world knew Esther Brite. They hummed her tunes, they fell in love while listening to her lyrics, they danced and made love to her melodies. Her songs of courage and pride could make your skin tingle. When she wrote of love and life your heart felt light with hope. Her snappy tunes of joy and the little pleasures in life made your knees bounce with the rhythm.

Before he came to Bellewood, Esther Brite had been to Dan exactly who she was to everyone else: Seth Tobin's partner and wife. Seth had a strong, melodious voice and a charisma that compelled loyalty and devotion among all ages, sexes, and races.

Extremely good-looking, Seth carried a sexy attitude about him that had women swooning and dropping like flies. Oddly enough this didn't offend his male following. Men found him humble yet macho, a down-home kind of guy they felt they would be able to talk football with on any given Sunday afternoon.

Older people liked him because publicity surrounding his private life was quiet and guarded. He was never involved in scandals with drugs or found cavorting with women. He was the first to profess his love for his wife and admitted freely that he'd still be singing at county fairs and in bars if he hadn't met Esther Brite.

Seth and Esther seemed to fit together like a hand and glove. Seth was the glove—handsome, virile, a talented singer, and a magical performer. Esther was the hand that held the glove up. Strikingly beautiful, she was the musical genius behind Seth. She wrote the music and lyrics Seth sang. Together they were a perfect team, a complete talent. Their relationship was romanticized; they became America's sweethearts and had a strong following for over ten years.

The newspaper reporters had run amok with sordid

questions, however, when Seth and his ten-month-old son were killed in a car accident. Pictures of a shrouded Esther at her husband and baby's funeral were seen everywhere for days. Then there was nothing. Esther had gone into hiding—no one seemed to know where she was or what she was doing.

Dan Jacobey knew. Esther Brite was sleeping in his spare bedroom fighting for her life . . . again. For Dan, she had started out as a talented musician and lyricist. He'd admired her work and sung the choruses to her songs, just like everyone else. It wasn't until after he came to Bellewood that she'd become so alive and so tangible to him that he'd allowed himself to fall in love with the woman she was inside.

At first he'd found it mildly interesting that such a huge success story had started in the little mining town of Bellewood. Then he'd met and cared for Esther's mother. A small frail woman, she was consumed with disease. It affected not only her body, but her mind. Laura had talked to Esther, among others, as her mind wandered over the years, in and out of reality. Dan gleaned volumes of information about the famous Esther from Laura, from Addy Markham, and from the other people of Bellewood.

It wasn't until after he'd decided to stay in Bellewood for a while that he discovered he'd become obsessed with her. He bought Laura Brite's house from the company bank, but hadn't been so far gone as to turn it into a shrine to Esther. He was a man who liked comfort and pleasure, and the house was too stark for him. And thank God for that, he realized, because if he hadn't decided to remodel, he might never have found out who Esther really was. He would never have found . . .

"Doc?" Esther's voice broke into his reverie from far away. "Doc?"

"Yes," he replied, then cleared his throat.

"Sorry," she said sleepily. "I thought maybe you'd fallen asleep there. Is anything wrong?"

"No," Dan said, pushing himself away from the door-jamb and crossing the room to her. Automatically he took up her wrist and counted the pulse beats. "How are you feeling?"

"Better. Really washed out, but better," she told him, trying to read his expression through the darkness. Quiet and stern, he was a strange man to decipher. No one with hands so gentle, with eyes so guarded and intense could be so surly. Maybe it was her. Maybe he didn't like her personally.

"Good," he said approvingly. "Can I get you anything? More water?"

"How about a new nurse?" she asked jokingly, trying to defuse the tension between them.

"What's wrong with Addy?" he asked bluntly, no humor in his tone.

"I think she has a crush on my doctor," Esther said, determined to see the man smile again. "She read me the riot act this morning for being rude to you. She says I owe you a lot and that I should behave myself."

"She's right," Dan's tone was still controlled, even though he wanted to kiss her and hold her tight and tell her how brave and strong and wonderful she was.

"I'll try," Esther promised. "She . . . ah . . . she also told me how kind you were to my mother. I wanted to thank you."

"Your mother was a nice lady. I was sorry I couldn't do more to help her," Dan stated simply, wondering if now was a good time to deliver Laura's message. "She was very proud of you."

Esther nodded. She knew how much her mother had loved her; she'd reconciled herself to it long ago. Esther had tried to help her mother. She'd sent money, but her mother had refused to use it. She'd coerced her mother into taking a trip to California to see her and Seth accept their first Grammy. The woman had practically run all the way back to the train station, she'd been so eager to get back to Bellewood. Esther had chosen not to attend the funeral because returning to Bellewood wouldn't have eased her grief at the loss of her mother, and at that point her mother wouldn't have known the difference.

"Call if you need anything," Dan said.

Esther looked up and could feel his deep brown eyes watching her with what might have been concern, but he turned abruptly and strode to the door.

"Dr. Jacobey," Esther called. "Thank you."

Dan looked over his shoulder at the woman he knew better than any other woman alive. "You're welcome," he said in the voice of a perfect stranger.

Esther spent the entire next week in bed, dozing and eating and napping and, when the opportunity presented itself, doubling her efforts to bring a smile to the grumpy physician's lips.

She found herself looking forward to his rare appearances. She liked watching his long fingers deftly go about their work. She sat calmly and studied his face while he took her pulse. His hair was dark brown and straight, but there was a body to it that made it curl at the ends along his neck and around his ears. He wore it swept back away from his face, so she easily could take in his strong features—the straight brows over his too-serious eyes, his thick lashes and full lips. When he spoke, she could see straight white teeth and would wish again that he'd smile at her.

But what she really anticipated, twice a day, was the hesitation she felt in him before he listened to her lungs with his stethoscope. The fact that he was reluctant to touch her bare skin was very undoctorlike, and it intrigued her. First to admit she was no expert on men, his uncertainty made Esther feel heady. In her marriage to Seth, which had been based on mutual respect and compatability, she had sensed the same exited hesitation at times. Seth had explained it as an overload of physical need, a fear of getting carried away to the point of hurting her. But that would in no way explain the doctor's odd behavior, she realized.

Unable to resist the temptation, she allowed far more of her firm, ripe breasts to touch his hand and arm than probably was necessary when she inhaled at his command. When he helped her sit up so he could listen through her back, she'd lean into him a little more than she needed to for support. His hands would tremble slightly, and Esther would wonder if he could feel her breasts swell and begin to tingle when he brushed against them. And why was it he never mentioned the erratic rhythm of her heart when he listened to it? These excitement-induced sensations she encountered while trying to evoke some sort of response from Dr. Indifferent were addictive. She enjoyed the thrill of knowing that she was getting to him, but she also knew she shouldn't behave so wantonly simply to fluster him. It was no way to repay his kindness, but she couldn't help herself. She was accustomed now to being noticed. Not that he ignored her. He was polite in his own rough way, but there was no sign of attraction, no sign of real dislike, just an apathy that was driving Esther nuts.

"You're clearing up nicely," he informed her coolly. They discussed the frequency of her bronchospasms briefly before he announced, "You can sit in the chair today. If you do well, you can walk out and watch television tomorrow or the next day."

"Great," Esther said. "Can I get up now?"

Dan thought about waiting for Addy to help her, but the woman was old. He couldn't expect *Addy* to do everything for Esther just because *he* enjoyed touching her too much.

He threw back her sheets and died a thousand deaths to see how high her nightgown had crawled up her thighs. With superhuman control he slipped an arm behind her and helped her to sit up over the edge of the bed.

She reached up a hand and grabbed the front of his shirt, and he watched as her eyes closed.

"I think I'm going to pass out."

"No, you won't. Sit there a minute till the light-headedness passes. Your blood's used to lower altitudes," he explained calmly.

It wasn't long before her green and gold eyes looked up in relief to meet his and she nodded her readiness.

He eased her off the bed, and she took several steps toward the chair in the corner of the room before her knees buckled under her. She slipped gently to the floor, Dan slowing her fall, and landed on her knees. Dan took a firmer grip and in one swift, effortless motion he brought her up into his arms.

For several seconds, they stared deeply into each others' eyes, tense and anxious at what they might find. He cradled her in his arms close to his heart and rejected each passing moment as a good opportunity to put her in the chair. More than anything he wanted to keep her in his arms, protect her, never let pain touch her again.

Esther was suddenly paralyzed with fear. What had she been thinking of in teasing this man? He was extremely dangerous. His dark eyes searched her face as if he were trying to unlock her emotions. His gentle touch and warm, strong body were bringing to life feelings she'd put to sleep long ago. His breath mingled with hers, entered her body and went seeking sensations so dangerous, she'd had to banish them totally to keep them from destroying her. And yet . . . she felt an allure to court this danger, she sensed a oneness with him that started somewhere near the beginning of time and stretched out past eternity. It was very strange, wondrous.

"You're nothing but skin and bones," Dan said absently. "You're far too thin."

"My hair is probably a mess too," Esther complained, suddenly feeling self-conscious and badly lacking as a woman.

"No," he said, looking her over with great interest, "it's . . . not," he finished, and placed her carefully in the overstuffed armchair.

To bridge the silence, Dan made a great production of covering her lap and legs with an afghan and her shoulders with a small blanket.

"When I packed up your things at the motel to bring them here, there was a hairbrush. Would you like to have it?" he asked, recalling how he'd held it and studied the inlaid wood pattern on the back, wondering if Seth had given it to her. It had obviously been well used and cared for.

Addy had brushed her long dark hair for her yesterday until it was smooth and shiny, but Esther's hand automatically went up to check the damage of a night's sleep.

"It's there on the table," she told him quietly, and watched as he picked it up, studying it briefly before handing it to her.

"This was a gift from Addy on my sixteenth birthday," she informed him. "It seems like forever ago," she added before making a passive swipe at her hair.

It was obvious to them both that she still wasn't strong enough to brush her own hair. "Would you like me to brush it for you this time?" Dan offered reluctantly.

Esther lowered her eyes, feeling weak and useless. "Would you mind?"

"Not at all," he said breezily, aware that the tips of his fingers were tingling.

Dan brushed Esther's hair gently, absorbed in the task. Esther sat silent, enjoying the soothing sensations and wishing his fingers would touch her face more often.

"Where did you go after the accident?" he asked out of the blue, unable to stop himself, stunning Esther.

"I went to Europe first," she told him after a brief

pause. "Europeans are more familiar with Seth than with me, and I could walk around freely without being asked a lot of questions. When I came back I went to New England. People are polite and reserved and tend to mind their own business in Vermont. Seth . . . we owned a small farm up there. It was a pretty good hideout," she said, purposely ending on a cheerful note.

If it was because he hadn't asked her a personal question before or because he seemed genuinely interested as opposed to merely curious, Esther couldn't tell, but she felt good talking to him, instinctively knowing their conversation would go no further.

"Is that why you came back to Bellewood? To stay hidden away?" he asked, stroking her hair with care.

Esther laughed. It was a soft lilting sound Dan enjoyed very much. She should laugh more often, he decided.

"I claimed temporary insanity when Addy asked me that question, but I really don't know why I came. I remember being in New York with my agent. That's where I caught my cold; it was terrible. Anyway, the next thing I knew I was looking for something—something important—and the last time I remembered seeing it, it was here. Sounds really strange, doesn't it?" she said.

"You didn't bring much with you. I couldn't even find a coat," he told her, withholding his judgment of her behavior.

She laughed again. "Looking back, I must have been feverish then, too, because I was burning up in my sweater and decided not to bring a coat."

"You need a keeper," he muttered under his breath.

"Are you volunteering," she asked flippantly, then quietly waited for his answer.

"No," he said, handing her brush back to her. "I'd rather see you do it for yourself."

Esther frowned. Suddenly his demeanor was suspicious and accusing, and she had no idea why.

"You're mad because I caught a cold?" she asked dubiously.

"I'm mad because you didn't take care of yourself and almost died," he answered reproachfully.

"Do you think I got sick on purpose? That I'm trying to kill myself? That I don't want to live anymore?" Esther questioned, her anger overriding her amazement.

"Tell me what I should think."

"You should think I'm human, that I made a mistake. I've made lots of them in my time," she told him firmly, leaving no room for him to doubt her mental stability. Then, struck by inspiration, she added in a softer tone, "Or you could think I just needed an excuse to meet you."

Caught off guard, Dan studied her closely for several seconds before he grinned, his eyes twinkling with good humor.

"It's lovely," said Esther, taking her turn at being vulnerable.

"What?"

"Your smile," she said, smiling back. "It's one of the nicest I've ever seen. I hope I'll get to see it more often."

"We'll see how rapidly you recover," he said cautiously, moving back into his role as doctor, but still smiling. "I get a little hard to live with when things don't go the way I want them to. Are you tired, or would you like to stay up a little longer?"

"I'd like Addy to see me. She expressed some concern yesterday about my taking root in bed," Esther replied lightly. "Besides, I can sleep almost as well here as I do in the bed. Sleeping is one of the things I do best."

"Okay. I have some paperwork to do. I'll be down the hall if you change your mind." With that, he left.

Esther closed her eyes wearily. When she opened them, they were trained on the floor where she remembered the loose plank to be. Did it still creak loudly when stepped on? Surely the nail had been removed when the carpet had been laid, but had they discovered the loose board?

She looked up to find a large, green-eyed tabby cat sitting in the doorway. A small black mole, obviously his get-well present to her, lay dead at his feet.

Esther curled her lip in disgust. "You're very handsome, but you're crude and sadly lacking in social graces."

The cat seemed most pleased to hear this. He picked up his prize, pranced across the floor, and placed it at her feet.

"You're too kind, you murderous feline," Esther said to the cat, patting her lap.

The cat responded promptly by leaping to her lap, leaving his catch on the floor. He padded around a little and, finding her lap not too bony, curled up contentedly and allowed Esther to pet him.

"I thought you were talking to me," Dan said from the doorway. "His name's Jasper. He usually stays outside. Even when the weather is rotten and cold."

"Well, Jasper is visiting the sick today and bearing gifts of joy," Esther informed him disdainfully, pointing to the mole on the floor but not looking at it.

Dan grimaced and disappeared, returning with a dustpan and broom.

"He means well," Dan explained as he swept the small dead animal into the pan and took it out of the room.

Esther closed her eyes and ran her hand over Jasper's fur.

She still tired too easily, Dan noted with concern when he returned. Her color was better, though, and her cough less harsh. All she needed now was time and a little loving care. He stood watching her until her hand stilled and fell limply on the cat's body. He assumed they were both asleep when he moved away to return to his work.

"Why are you doing this?" Esther asked softly, her eyes still closed.

"What?" Dan wanted to know, feeling foolish for having stood so long watching her.

"You could have taken me to Fairmont, but you brought me here instead. I'm not a company dependent anymore. You don't have to treat me."

"I know," he admitted. "I wanted to."

"Why?"

"You're ill. I'm a doctor. I want to help you get well. It's as simple as that," he said.

Esther opened her eyes and looked searchingly at him. She felt there was more to his kindness than just professionalism but couldn't think of a way to force his confession. She nodded her temporary defeat but made it clear his answer was inadequate.

"I need to call and let my agent know where I am," she said, coolly changing the subject.

"If it can wait another day, there's a phone in my study or in the kitchen you can use. But I'd rather you didn't overdo it today," he said, his own tone slightly placating. "I could call for you if you'd like."

Esther shook her head. "It can wait," she said, then closed her eyes dismissively.

Dan, realizing she was a little annoyed with him, went back to his study full of frustration. What was he supposed to do? Throw himself at her feet, proclaiming his undying love, and let her laugh in his face? No way.

Three

As a child Esther had been so accustomed to the constant humming from the mines that for the most part, she hadn't really heard it. But she could hear it now and took comfort in knowing the closer one got to the mines, the louder and more distinct the noises became until the humming finally disappeared and one recognized the individual sounds of the trucks and machinery. It was a relief to perceive something and feel sure of its cause and effect.

The feelings churning within her were not as easy to identify. She felt their effect in the unsettled and dissatisfied way she'd been floundering about in her life lately, but she was still unsure of the cause. It seemed to Esther that nothing was as it should be. Every step she had taken, every move she'd made since the accident had been cautious, timid. She was frightened all the time, and it was a feeling she was neither used to nor proud of.

Even in her mother's home nothing was the same. She knew it was stupid to think that her bedroom had been the only room changed, but she was surprised when she left her sickroom to find that the stark, gloomy house of her childhood had vanished. It had been replaced with a home decorated in warm earthy colors and plush furniture. The windows were larger, and the drapes pulled open to allow every available ray of sunlight to filter through the dark winter skies and into the house as if there were nothing to hide. The stale musty odors she could almost taste in recollection had been chased away with clean fresh air.

Dan had done a wonderful job of remodeling. His home was cozy and welcoming . . . but it was his home now, not hers. She felt rootless and vulnerable and suddenly out of place in a house where she'd spent half her life. It intimidated Esther, and she again began to question her wisdom in returning to Bellewood.

If the home she'd known inside and out as a child had changed so much, how much had the town changed? Were the answers she sought still here? If not . . . what then?

The Bellewood she'd left behind was a coal-mining, company town, one of the last towns in the country still privately owned. At one point in its history it had boasted of an even one thousand families drawing their livelihoods in one way or another from the mines. But that was well before her time. Over the years, the Great Depression, the mechanization of the coal-mining in-dustry, the dawn of modern technology, and the de-cline in the demand for coal all took their toll.

Isolated in the hills of northern West Virginia, the town and the mines were dying, and had been since Esther was a young girl. But the people who remained, generation after generation, were employed coal min-ers. The key word being *employed*.

The United Mine Workers had done much to improve the working conditions of miners. This included good wages for their perilous occupation—when they worked. She could remember that shutdowns and layoffs had occurred often with the fluctuation in the demand for coal, with mechanical failures, and with poor weather conditions. The result was an unstable economy. The miner's plight, it was taken by all as a fact of life. They worked hard when they could and prayed each layoff would be a short one.

As an adult looking back, Esther had to admit that Bellewood was probably like most small towns in being tightly knit and devoted to its traditions. The same people had shown up at the same events on the same dates year after year. They knew one another's lineage, they compensated for one another's idiosyncrasies, and they forgot nothing. A stranger in their midst tended to upset this delicate balance with excitement and suspicion alike. Had this been the case when the handsome, young unmarried doctor, Dan Jacobey, had come to town? He also appeared to have a mysterious past, or so one would think, as he obviously was overtrained for the position of general practitioner. Esther couldn't help but wonder about him, about his past and what kept him in Bellewood.

She wondered, too, how the people of Bellewood felt about her return. She could remember that the occasional child of this tiny township who had endeavored to attend college, providing the funds could be raised, or sought a better life outside Bellewood had not been forgotten when he chose not to return. Rather, that child had been asked about frequently, discussed and remembered openly, and more often than not claimed as one of the town's success stories.

Had Esther Brite been one of those children? Had her fame and fortune done anything to haze over the memory of her lowly beginnings in Bellewood? Did they ever ask about her? Was she one of their success stories? And why on earth do I care what they think anyway, Esther asked herself with a shake of her head and a heavy sigh as she tried to focus her attention on the checker game she and Dan were involved in.

"Crown me," Dan ordered as he pushed a black

checker to Esther's side of the board, grinning smugly. Then, noting her sigh and sad expression, he asked, "What's wrong?"

"You're an obnoxious winner, that's what's wrong. I thought doctors were supposed to be merciful," Esther complained as she placed one of her hard-won black checkers atop his.

"And you, beautiful, are a rotten loser," Dan said in a cocky voice.

Esther brought her head up sharply. This was the first time he'd unguardedly called her anything but Esther or Miss Brite. Having seen herself in black and white, described in print as stunning, arresting, glamorous, and so on, she was totally surprised to feel a warm blush crawl up her neck. Her embarrassment turned the flush to a hot throbbing sensation in her face. How foolish she was to be so moved by his careless compliment, she realized.

Dan looked up expectantly. "Your move," he said, then added again, "Now what's wrong?"

"I think that's the nicest thing you've said to me in three weeks," Esther replied.

"What? That you're beautiful?"

Esther nodded.

"I told you yesterday you had a good strong pulse and excellent recuperative powers," he said teasingly as he took in the rosiness of her cheeks. His muscles tensed when he saw the wonder in her eyes.

She was charming, just as he knew she would be, natural and unassuming as if she hadn't spent half her life in the limelight. She was certainly not the same girl who had left Bellewood at the ripe old age of sixteen. She had seen and done much in her life and it showed. But she also retained many of the qualities of the young Esther—the humor, the will to survive, the intelligence, and the beauty of heart.

Over the past couple of weeks, with her increasing strength, she'd gently worn on Dan's reserve. More and more he found it impossible to guard his feelings from her. More and more he found himself responding to her allure. More and more he wanted to cross the final barriers and claim her as his own.

But not yet.

Esther was on a quest. Searching for answers or a meaning or a purpose, something only she would recognize when she found it. To complicate her life now would be unfair, even could be destructive.

"You're a prince among men," Esther retaliated, "and a real boost to any woman's ego. 'Eat this. Eat that. You're too skinny. You look pale. Take this, you're sick,' " she mimicked, harassing him good-naturedly.

"Which reminds me, we need to find you a coat and get some fresh air into you," he said, ignoring her taunts but enjoying her liveliness.

"How about this afternoon?" she suggested eagerly.

"Okay. Then we'll go over to the clinic so I can get a repeat chest X ray. Crown me again," he said, his attention back on the game.

Esther growled, crowned him, and made her move. Then she asked, "Why a chest X ray? I thought I was getting better?"

"Then we'll have proof positive." He jumped her twice, leaving two red checkers on the board.

"I suppose I'll need to leave then," she said more to herself than to Dan as she considered her next move—both on and off the board.

Dan frowned as his gaze focused on her. "No," he said abruptly and with more force than he'd intended. "You won't be completely well for months. And certainly not well enough to travel for several more weeks."

"I could stay at the motel for a while, I guess," she said, not seeing or hearing his concern. "Or at Addy's."

"Why?"

Glancing at him as if he'd suddenly become extremely obtuse, she couldn't help but laugh softly.

"This is Bellewood, remember?" she reminded him.

"Do you want to burn in hell forever for living with me out of wedlock? We both know it is under the most clinical circumstances, but don't you care about what people no doubt are beginning to think by now?"

"I don't know," Dan said, a slow, sly smile curling his lips. "There are some very hypotensive people in this town. Might do them a lot of good to have something to get stirred up about. It could be real therapeutic," he said. "I'm willing to continue this arrangement for Bellewood's sake, if you are."

Esther smiled, then shook her head. "I can't. I've imposed on you for too long. You've been very kind—once you got over that nastiness in the beginning—and I appreciate all you've done, but—"

Dan held up a hand to stop her, searching for the right words. "Esther, please don't go. Not yet. I know you came here for a reason, and I want to help." His fathomless brown eyes were sincere and pleading. "If you need privacy, I can stay at the clinic, but I think you should stay here, in your house. In fact, I insist on it. What I'm offering is my friendship. An ear to listen if you want to talk. A shoulder to cry on if you need to. I've come to care about you, and I want to be your friend."

Esther wasn't surprised by his offer. She'd seen how gentle and respectful of Addy he was, and she'd been told of some of his other kindnesses to the people of Bellewood. What startled her was the quiver of passion in his voice, the mesmerizing need in his eyes, the unfeigned honesty of his offer.

A great force rose within her, pushing aside good sense and old memories, propelling her forward with a momentum she knew would be useless to struggle against.

Tilting her head to one side, she contemplated the doctor's offer, then asked him quite frankly, "And would you kiss me if I asked?"

With his elbow resting on the arm of the chair, his

fist came up to support his chin as he gave her a single affirmative nod, his gaze intent, never wavering from hers.

Call it a whim, a need, or a driven compulsion, but Esther had no control over her next act. With her heart pounding, her voice hardly more than a whisper Esther asked, "Please kiss me, Dr. Jacobey."

Afraid this was just another of his dreams, Dan was reluctant to move or even blink for fear he'd wake up and she'd disappear again.

Slowly he extended the hand from under his chin in her direction, stretching the fingers until they met hers on the checkerboard. Their fingers intertwined, and with a firm but gentle pressure he drew her from her chair, around the table, and into his arms, never once breaking the bond their gazes had formed.

Esther allowed herself to be drawn onto his lap and into a loose embrace. As intense and boundless as his eyes appeared, there was also a reassuring solidness, a comforting stability about them. They reflected his personality—deep and strong, giving and intuitive. She was fiercely attracted to him and had thought of little else but kissing him for days now. So why was she quaking inside?

"Are you sure this is what you want, Esther?" he asked her in a low voice, giving her a chance to change her mind, knowing exactly what he himself wanted.

"I can't predict how I'll feel tomorrow, Dan, but right now I'd like very much to kiss you," Esther declared quietly as her hand moved to touch the soft brown hair that feathered back along the side of his head. Having studied it for so long, she knew how it would feel: soft and clean and thick.

But she hadn't expected the tingling in her muscles when she felt Dan's touch across her cheek and along her jaw. She hadn't expected his fingers to be so warm as they slid around the base of her neck. It was more than a little disconcerting to realize that the excitement she'd known before came not from the playing of a game but from the mere touch of his hands. Then she received an electrical jolt when his lips finally met hers in a tentative kiss.

Dan looked for her reaction in her unusual eyes and was overjoyed to see the curiosity that expressed itself so clearly. His anxiety and reluctance to live out his fantasy ebbed, and he became eager to see how she'd respond to a more intimate kiss.

Drawing her close again, he placed tiny kisses along her lower lip, lulling her before taking total possession of her mouth. He tasted her sweetness, teasing her senses until he felt her arms close around his neck with a fervor that matched his own.

When Dan moved to deepen the kiss, Esther gave freely, overtaken by a soul-soothing feeling of fulfillment. His lips and tongue lapped at her senses, scattering them in a thousand different directions at once. His hands moved over her body with a strength and gentleness her battered heart had been yearning for. He demanded that she give of herself, relinquish part of her inner being . . . and she gave . . . as much as she could.

When at last they separated, Esther's forehead came to rest on his while she waited for her world to right itself.

"Is this prescription refillable?" she asked, smiling her contentment.

"Absolutely," Dan muttered, squeezing her gently. "Anytime, anywhere."

They were silent for several minutes, refusing to release the moment, to let time move forward again. Suddenly Esther laughed.

"What's so funny?" Dan asked.

"I was just wondering what someone like you is doing in a place like this." She grinned at him.

"Isn't that my line?" Dan asked.

"Not in this case. I have a vague excuse. Your reason is a mystery."

"No mystery," he said calmly. "I just got sick of the city. I got tired of practicing metropolitan medicine."

"But why Bellewood, of all places?"

"I was needed here."

"It's that simple? No mystery?" she asked.

"No mystery," Dan confirmed, but found it very hard to meet her gaze and sound convincing at the same time. The truth wasn't a mystery, but it wasn't simple either. It was much more complicated and painful.

A friendly familiarity prevailed during their lunch hour, while Addy Markham fussed about, giving her opinion on nearly every subject under the sun.

"I caught Her Highness bad-mouthin' you in town this morning," Addy commented as she placed simple bowls of soup and sandwiches before both members of her audience. "I'd been wonderin' how long it'd take her to get to stirrin' things up around here again. Says you livin' with the doc is a bad example for her young Edgar and the other young people of Bellewood, as she calls 'em."

Addy's disdainful snort left Esther in little doubt as to whom she was speaking about. She'd heard the same sound a thousand times in years past and, fond as she was of it, her brow automatically furrowed with concern.

"Oh, Addy." Esther groaned. "I hope just this once you didn't bite off more than I can chew. I really don't feel up to coming to blows with Jewel Belldon today."

The old woman laughed reminiscently and winked at Dan before she spoke. "Ya won't have to bloody her nose again today; I tagged her a good one for ya. Told her she was mad cuz the doc wouldn't look twice at her but had you sleepin' in the room right next to his, and he was gettin' you healthier and stronger every day."

"Oh, Addy," Esther wailed, her skin warming at the

implications of Addy's words. She glanced over in Dan's direction to gauge his reaction, only to find a silly smirk on his face and his chest vibrating as he fought to swallow his laughter. "Don't encourage her," she told him, "you have no idea how much trouble this woman's blunt tongue has gotten me into."

"Yes, I do," Dan replied, finally letting his laughter loose, "she's told me. I've known for years how fond the Belldons are of you."

"And you still took me in?" she asked.

Dan shrugged. "They employ me. They don't own me."

"Will you two let me finish?" Addy broke in. "I want ya to know I fixed the woman's wagon. I told her the kids in this town ain't stupid. They got TV and they can see what some of their folks do when they need a little excitement in their lives. Said even her young Eddy could add and subtract. Him bein' sixteen and her bein' married sixteen years. Even a fool could figure out how his ma got to be a Belldon."

Esther groaned yet again and closed her eyes.

"Well, then I just told her if she hustled around and found another school to take him off her hands, she wouldn't have to worry about what he thinks of you and the doc. She don't deserve that boy anyway," Addy said decisively.

"What is he like?" Esther asked, suddenly curious.

"Mixed up, mostly. He's a tough little nut, but I think there's some real sweet meat inside if anyone ever felt like takin' the time to crack his shell," the old woman said.

Esther thought about this for a moment, then began to eat her lunch.

"Addy," she said casually between bites a short while later, "I'm all grown up now and I can fight my own battles from now on. I don't want you caught between the Belldons and me. Do you understand me?" she asked, her voice firm. She reached out to take Addy's hand and added, "I care about you. I don't want you hurt, especially on my account. They can't hurt me anymore."

Addy nodded silently, knowingly, and squeezed Esther's hand in return while Dan watched the exchange. He knew every thought, every emotion passing through Esther as she turned her gaze toward him.

"That goes for you too," Esther told Dan.

He nodded.

It was Dan's practice to hold office hours in the morning, have lunch at home—at which time he either sat and talked with Esther and Addy, or if Esther challenged him, played a quick game of cards or checkers—then make house calls in the afternoon.

This day was no different. Esther dressed and made herself presentable while Dan made his house calls to older miners who were restricted to bed with old age or the end stages of lung disease, and other patients unable to get into the office. She made a list of things she needed, vowing never to pack with a fever again. She'd brought several thick designer sweaters but only two pairs of slacks and a pair of jeans. She'd found two and a half pairs of shoes, none of which were appropriate for a West Virginia winter. Her list was long, but by the time Dan returned for her, it was fairly complete and she was ready to face Bellewood.

Located in a valley between two mountains and surrounded by even more, the town worked its way up a riverbank with two streets of row houses that stretched three-quarters of a mile, the entire length of Bellewood. There was, of course, a main street on which the town's commerce transpired, and beyond that and farther up the hill were three more rows of houses.

Laura Brite's home, and, of course, Addy Markham's, were located outside of the town proper. Laura's home had been built halfway up the side of the mountain, among the trees, on an access road leading to the mines. Addy's had been built before the mines existed and was around the mountainside and very isolated.

Bellewood, to Esther's relief, had changed little. Shabbier and more decayed than she remembered, she was glad to see that most of the homes along the river had been vacated. Naturally, there were die-hard people who preferred homes on the river. Unfortunately, the rents and mortgages on the houses here were lower, due to their poor condition, which appealed to single mothers on fixed incomes and the other more downtrodden members of the population.

When Dan parked his Bronco in front of the emporium where he and Esther planned to shop, she couldn't suppress the giggle that rose to her lips.

She laughed. "Will you look at that? They haven't changed the signs in the window for seventeen years."

"Yes, they have," Dan said. "That one over in the corner was new two months ago."

"If I were any other celebrity in the world, after we leave they'd put a sign in the window saying Esther Brite shopped here," she said and smiled.

"Don't underestimate these people. They're very proud of your success," he informed her, realizing how anxious she must be feeling. This was her first real look into the past with a clear mind.

"Surprised by it is probably more the case," she replied skeptically. She released the latch and got out of the car.

Slowly she climbed the steps, and when she reached the portico, she turned to survey the town. It wasn't much, but what there was of it all belonged to the Belldons, whose large estate had been carved into the woods of the Allegheny Mountains in a higher valley several miles outside Bellewood.

Esther carried a cold resentment in her heart for the Belldon family. Old Edgar, a brilliant businessman who played the mines conservatively, drawing out their productivity and reaping their highest yields at the same time, had taken over the mines from his father, the original owner. Edgar was an invertebrate coward in Esther's mind. His son, the present owner, on the other hand, was a pompous, self-righteous fiend, inflicted on the world by a freak disaster of nature.

Esther couldn't help feeling a little sorry for the once-envied Jewel Avery, a tormentor from her childhood who had married young Tommy Belldon under scandalous circumstances the summer after Esther had left town. Young marriages in Bellewood were frequent and usually stormy. With Tommy Belldon, it must have been sheer hell. Esther easily forgave Jewel her derogatory remarks of that morning. If Jewel still had nothing better to talk about than Esther, she must be a very bitter woman after all these years.

"Ready?" asked Dan, his fingers wrapped reassuringly around her elbow.

Esther nodded and turned, but stopped dead when she saw a motorcyclist swoop down the street at breakneck speed. She watched him pass in front of her, turn down the block, and come back.

It was all she could do to squelch the nausea and the sensation of déjà vu that enveloped her. The cyclist pulled his bike in alongside Dan's Bronco and sat revving the engine, staring back at Esther through the darkened shield of his helmet.

Dressed totally in black leather astride a big black motorcycle, he was like an evil phantom from her past. Esther felt transported back in time and powerless as she watched him remove his helmet.

The fact that he was a Belldon descendant was evident from his straight black hair and the cocky, one-sided smile he wore on his face. He didn't bear much resemblance to his mother at all, except for the thinness of his nose. Everything about him, even the way he carried his tall, thin frame was reminiscent of his father.

"Your dad used to ride a bike like that one," Esther called out over the loud engine, hoping that if she talked to him, he'd become more real to her, less ghostly.

The boy cut the engine before saying, "I know. It's still out in the garage."

Esther nodded and turned back to Dan, who had remained tense and silent at her side.

"You're Esther Brite, aren't you?" the boy said.

Slowly Esther turned back around.

"Yes," she answered, braced for whatever would come next.

"I like most of your songs. I heard 'em at school and on the radio. Your tapes aren't allowed at our house," he said placidly.

Esther waited for his next comment.

"You better now?" he asked.

"Yes. Thanks," she replied automatically.

The boy nodded. Then, as if recalling his manners, he said, "I'm Ed Belldon."

"I figured that," Esther said with a polite smile.

"Did your mother talk to you about me before she died?" he asked bluntly.

"Only about your existence. Why? Were you friends?"

"No. Not really," he admitted as he looked down the street in the direction in which he had been headed. Remembering his purpose, he said to Esther, "I gotta go. Are you staying in town awhile?"

"I'm not sure," she said vaguely.

"Well," he shouted as he started his bike up again, "I'll probably see you around."

He replaced his helmet, backed the bike up with his feet, and sped off, oblivious to the wet state of the road.

"Charming young man," Esther commented.

"Hmm," was Dan's dubious sound of agreement.

Esther entered the store with considerable trepidation. While she and Dan moved from aisle to aisle shopping for the things on her list, they encountered several people Esther remembered who called her by name and politely asked about her health. A few expressed their enjoyment of her music; several young women who had been in high school when they last saw her felt compelled to tell her who they'd married and how busy their careers as mothers kept them.

Dan tuned in sharply when the chitchat centered around marriages and children. She hadn't talked about the accident, and he wasn't sure how sensitive Esther's wounds still were. She seemed pleased enough with the reception she received and cheerfully congratulated the mothers on their progeny. In fact, he was rather proud of the way she was handling things. In general, the good citizens of Bellewood had treated Esther like dirt until she was sixteen and was forced to leave town. Now that she was someone wonderful in their eyes she was politely reserved in her response, not cold as she had the right to be, and not hot as if the past never existed, but warm and friendly, approachable, and special unto herself.

With Esther's shopping done, Dan took the packages out to the car while she finished talking to an old miner who felt obliged to recall fond memories of his mining days.

When the elegant black Continental pulled up across the street and Tom Belldon got out, Dan's emotions went on alert. Should he go in and hustle Esther out or should he hold back and let her handle her own problems as she'd asked, he wondered.

"Doctor" was the mine owner's condescending acknowledgment before he mounted the steps and walked boldly into the emporium.

Dan's conscience settled in midfield. He climbed the steps lightly and crossed to sit on a cold bench where he could listen through the door that Belldon had left slightly ajar. If Esther needed him, he'd be there.

"Esther," Tom Belldon said in a commanding voice.

Esther knew the voice. It was a little more mature and slightly deeper but basically unchanged. She turned her head and looked at Tom Belldon, slowly taking in his tall, thin frame, straight dark hair, and icy blue eyes which had retained their gelid quality over the years and still had the power to make her shiver. With great deliberation she turned back to the old miner to finish their discussion.

The man may have been old but he wasn't senile. He'd worked for the Belldons a long time and could read them very well. The conversation came to a friendly but abrupt end.

Other customers moved away quietly as well, but were careful to remain within hearing distance.

Masking her face to hide her emotions, refusing to allow the fifteen-year-old girl in her to tremble in fear and anger, Esther headed for the door.

"The boy told me you were finally out and about. I was beginning to think the good doctor was keeping you prisoner and all to himself," he said calmly in a superior, taunting tone. "Every time I've tried to see you, he's refused me, saying you weren't taking visitors."

"I'll have to remember to thank him," Esther said just as calmly, just as superior and in no less taunting a tone.

"It's been a long time," he said.

"Not long enough, Tommy," she stated firmly.

"When are you leaving town?"

"When I'm ready."

"You're not welcome here, Esther. All this town holds for you is more pain. Go back to California. You don't belong here anymore," he told her. He crossed his arms over his chest in a manner denoting authority, and as he did, the sleeve of his jacket rode up his arm to reveal a circular scar on his wrist.

The scar was old and had faded back to his normal skin tone. In fact, it was hardly visible. But Esther spotted it and took a certain amount of joy remember-

ing that it had become infected and that he'd under-
gone a considerable amount of therapy for it. Her lips
curled in a knowing smile when he caught her staring
at it and quickly lowered his arms.

"Have I made myself clear?"

"Perfectly. How's Jewel?" she asked, ignoring his
threat.

Tom Belldon's eyes narrowed in anger as he scruti-
nized her. "Let's just say she's not getting the mileage
out of the mines that you got out of Seth Tobin."

"Meaning?"

"Meaning you and your mother and my wife are three
of a kind," he said snidely.

Esther gave her head a hopeless shake and looked at
Tom in disbelief.

"Poor Jewel," she said, "stuck with a man and a
town that just grow older and more rundown every
year. Give her my sympathy, will you, Tommy?" Esther
pulled the door open and saw Dan standing tensely on
the other side. She flashed him a quick smile of reassurance and walked to the car. She wanted to run, to
run as she had that night so many years ago, but she
kept each step slow and measured. She reminded herself that she wasn't the innocent she once was. She
possessed a personal power now that no one, not even
Tommy Belldon, could take from her. He may have
shaken her up a little, but it wouldn't happen again,
she resolved.

Four

The trip to Dan's clinic was made in silence. Esther had no desire to discuss what had transpired with Tom Belldon. If trouble was brewing, she didn't want Dan involved. Her past was *her* past and none of Dan's concern. Oh, she knew he'd probably heard stories about her over the last few years, and she could feel his questioning, curious glances now as they drove along Main Street. But the truth was best left unsaid. For his sake . . . and for the sake of her pride.

The company clinic was small but remarkably well equipped. Esther was impressed with the airy, modern decor, its roominess, and the atmosphere of being in a real medical facility. There was even a whole room full of X-ray equipment which Dan explained helped considerably not only in diagnosing the early stages of lung disease in the miners, but also in the setting of broken bones sustained in mining accidents. In the past Doc Evans had treated patients as best he could manage before they were referred elsewhere or given up on.

While Dan went on to tell about the initial expense of

the equipment versus the long-run savings in medical expenses to the company, Esther couldn't help but notice the detached impersonal way he was speaking. It was almost as if the past two weeks hadn't happened and he was still the cold, brusque professional doctor she had first met. When he pressed his hands against her shoulders to position her for the X ray—knowing she was naked above the waist except for a thin paper drape—his hands were steady and his manner very businesslike.

Her disappointment grew after he told her to get dressed. Not only had he not looked twice at her nearly naked body, but he hadn't tried to touch her in the least familiar way. Feeling rejected and confused, she dressed and went out to join him in the reception area where he was waiting impatiently to leave.

"Well?" Esther asked, irritated by his sudden cold-shoulder treatment.

"Well, what?" he asked absently as if nothing were wrong.

"Are you going to tell me what's wrong, or are you enjoying your blue funk?"

"I'm not in a funk and there's nothing wrong."

"Coulda fooled me," she muttered to his back as he moved to leave the clinic, his stride long and purposeful.

"Come on, Esther. You've had a long day. I don't want you getting too tired your first day out," he said, not bothering to look in her direction.

He stepped aside and allowed her to pass through the door in front of him so he could check the security of the lock. But he still managed to have the engine started and the Bronco in motion before Esther had her seat belt buckled.

The rest of the evening didn't fare much better for Esther. In so many words he instructed her to "go to bed." He had proceeded to his den and closed the door, effectively shutting her out. Dinner was a torturous melody of forks scraping plates and the sounds of two people chewing meat.

After they'd finished eating, Esther challenged Dan to a game of cards or checkers. He refused, claiming he was behind on his reading. Esther got the distinct impression that she'd disappointed him somehow, that he'd withdrawn from her and the reading was just an excuse to get away from her.

She did the dishes alone and later went to her room and removed the tags from her new clothing—none of which were the top designer brands that usually occupied her closets. Then again, she realized, things like that hadn't ever really mattered to her. What had been important was that she had the *ability* to buy what she wanted, when she wanted it, whether it was cheap or expensive.

She tried to read for a short while herself, but her thoughts kept straying down the hall to Dan's study at the rear of the house. She missed him, missed the sharing and caring they'd had earlier in the day, missed his presence in the room.

Not since the day she'd left Bellewood had Esther let an unsolved problem dangle so long. And she wasn't about to start now. Determinedly she snapped the book closed and made her way to the door of the study. It was open. She could see Dan standing by the small window holding the curtain aside, staring solemnly out into the night.

"Good book?" she asked.

Dan turned slowly, looking a bit sheepish. "I couldn't concentrate."

"Why not? What's wrong?" she asked, her expression concerned.

Dan sighed indecisively as he gazed at her intently. He took a quick step forward, stopped, then held both hands out and tried to explain.

"It's none of my business, Esther. I'm trying very hard not to get involved. I just can't help it."

"What isn't?"

"You. Your life. How you live it," he replied vaguely.

"What's wrong with my life?" she asked.

Dan sighed again, lifted his hands, and let them fall. "Why the hell didn't you punch his lights out?" he asked in an angry rush.

"Whose?"

"Tom Belldon's," he shouted. Knowing that she had only half the picture, Dan visibly tried to calm himself. Slowly he crossed the room to her and grasped her hand in a warm and caring way. Leading her to the couch, he began his story.

"I know all about you, Esther." His voice was gentle and truthful. "I know about you, and your mother and father; about Tom and Jewel Belldon. I know why you left here when you were only sixteen years old. I know about the deal that was made that's kept you quiet and out of the way all this time." He paused briefly. "I probably shouldn't, but I do."

Aside from Tom Belldon, there was only one other person alive who knew the truth about her, and Addy Markham wouldn't have discussed it even with Tom. She searched his face for his thoughts, his judgment on her past, but saw no negative emotions. There was no pity or condemnation in his expression, only concern and respect.

"Did Mama tell you?" she asked, her throat tight from the rush of feelings that had assaulted her after Dan's confession.

Dan couldn't meet her gaze. Instead, he took in the whiteness of her knuckles as she gripped his hand tightly.

"Not all of it . . . but then, she didn't know all of it, did she?" he asked softly. He looked back into her eyes, seeing her pain and confusion. He got to his feet and looked down at her, longing to hold her and soothe her, wanting to kiss away the humiliation she'd carried for so long.

"I . . . I know you weren't doing jumping jacks in your room the other day," he said as he moved to his desk and opened a drawer. "You were checking to see if the planking under the rug was still loose. You were wondering if this was still hidden underneath it," he said, producing a spiral notebook and holding it out to her.

With loving, reverent hands she took the old notebook and pressed it tightly between them. Tears welled in her eyes and she bit her quivering lower lip as she gazed at it in awe.

"My diary," she uttered on a soft breath.

"I found it four years ago. I . . . I guess I should have mailed it to you, but . . ." He couldn't tell her he'd treasured it for all this time, that he'd read it so often he knew it by heart. He had intruded on her life, invaded her most private thoughts, and he felt miserable for it now.

"You read it," she stated unquestioningly, feeling more naked and vulnerable than if he'd suddenly torn off all her clothes.

He nodded. "Yes. I'm sorry, Esther. It was irresistible at the time . . . which isn't a good enough excuse, I know, but I did read it and . . . I'm very sorry for the intrusion."

Dan was so beside himself with guilt that Esther wasn't sure who she felt worse for, him or herself.

"Better you than a reporter from the tabloids, I guess," she said only half jokingly. "You'd be a rich man if you'd sold it to them."

"I couldn't have," he told her, relieved that she didn't hate him for what he'd done. "I was very moved by it, Esther. It became very special to me. That's why I didn't mail it after I'd read it. I wanted to keep it."

Esther was beginning to feel very self-conscious over his truthfulness and the fact that he knew so much about her—more than her own husband had ever known.

"Maybe I should get it published," she said with a laugh, feeling extremely awkward.

"Well, at least the parts about the Belldons. I think the world ought to know what kind of slime they are," he said vehemently. "That's why I was so mad when you didn't stomp all over that creep this afternoon. Who the hell does he think he is, ordering you out of town?"

"He's scared," Esther explained almost sympathetically.

"Damn him," Dan practically spat out. "And you weren't scared seventeen years ago?"

"He's not me," she said simply. "I had the whole world waiting for me. All he has is Bellewood."

"Dammit, Esther, don't cut that bastard any slack. He tried to rape you."

"I'm the bastard, remember?" she reminded him with another nervous laugh. "And he didn't know I was his sister at the time."

"What difference does that make?" Dan asked. "What he did was brutal and disgusting. He shouldn't have gotten away with it."

"Oh, I think he paid for trying to teach me a lesson. Today I saw his keepsake from that night. Believe me, it's still very sensitive," Esther said in a satisfied tone.

Dan frowned and looked at her in disbelief. "What lesson was he trying to teach you? Not that it matters," he said, throwing his arms up in amazement. "What he did was inexcusable, but I'm just curious."

"It's hard to explain. I think it really bothered Tom that I wasn't ever humble enough or ashamed of myself because I had no father. I knew what I was, but I always had these dreams of being someone special. After a while I started believing I was special. It became a protective barrier for me. People could say what they pleased and it didn't hurt as much, because deep down I knew I was someone terrific.

"Actually the only time it really hurt was when they

said things to Mama and made her cry. That's why when Tom found he couldn't humiliate me into my place, he threatened to go after Mama and her job. Everyone knew the best way to get to me was through Mama."

Dan stared at her for a long time. She was special and terrific and too forgiving. It bothered him that she was so willing to rationalize all her past injuries.

"So now that your mother's gone, they can't hurt you, is that it? You're going to let Tom Belldon look down his nose at you and treat you like trash. And even though you know he's your brother, you're not going to try to teach him a lesson of your own?"

"No. I'm not going to let him do that to me anymore," Esther said earnestly. "But I'm also not going to go out looking for a fight. The way I feel about my past didn't come to me overnight. When I left here I was angry and bitter and so full of hatred. It takes a lot of energy to maintain those kinds of emotions. As far as I'm concerned, Bellewood and Tom Belldon are small potatoes in my life. They're not worth the energy it would take to make them pay for what they did so long ago."

Esther wasn't willing to admit she was still vulnerable, certainly not like she had been, but deep inside, the young girl in her was still hurting.

Dan was struggling to see her viewpoint. "You're a far better person than I am, Esther. I think if I'd gone as far as you have, coming from your background, I'd be looking for blood about now. Revenge would do my heart good."

"They say it leaves a bitter taste in your mouth," Esther reminded him.

"Maybe," he said reluctantly. "But I still think Tom Belldon has a lot of nerve treating you like he did today. The very least he could do now is keep a civil tongue in his head, and so help me God, Esther, if he—"

"Shh," Esther said as she stood and placed a silencing finger against his lips. "See now, this is exactly what I warned you against this afternoon at lunch. I don't want you mixed up in the situation. It's my problem and I can handle it." She paused thoughtfully. "I think it's wonderful that you want to come to my defense, but it really isn't necessary. I don't want blood and I don't want revenge. Neither one would make my life any better than it already is."

"What do you want, Esther?" Dan asked quietly as if her answer meant everything in the world to him.

"I . . . I just want to go on with my life. I came back here looking for something, but it doesn't have anything to do with the Belldons. It has to do with me," she said frankly, still feeling strange that he knew her secrets but also aware of how easy it was to talk to him about all of it.

"Can I do anything to help? Professionally . . . or personally?"

"What I would like from you is another kiss if you have an extra one lying around somewhere," she said longingly.

Not a sexually aggressive person normally, Esther found it extremely easy to express her desires to Dan. More than anything, she wanted to feel secure and comforted in his arms. When they first met, she'd been forced to trust this man with her life and now it seemed she was also to trust him with her deepest secrets and her pride. If her diary had to be found by anyone, she was almost glad and certainly relieved it had been Dan, because even unconsciously she knew she could trust him.

Dan's hands fell forward and landed loosely on her hips. Her eyes twinkled with happiness and contentment. Their greenness shone with a resiliency that sprang from her soul. Her spirit was still as indomitable as a sixteen-year-old's.

"Do you always end vigorous discussions like this?" he asked, fighting the grin that would be his downfall.

"Is that what that was? A vigorous discussion?" She laughed. "Yes. When I want to have the final word on any given subject, I sometimes have to resort to devious tactics."

"I'll remember that. Next time it won't be as easy for you."

"Well, it hasn't proven to be all that easy so far," she said. "Are you going to kiss me or talk all night?"

Her last word came on a rush of air as Dan grabbed her up in a fierce embrace and kissed her long and hard with a passion so great the hard muscles of his shoulders and legs trembled. He held her close, as if he were trying to make her a part of him.

Esther felt herself drawn quickly to the emotions generated by Dan's hungry kisses and possessive hands. They were strong, powerful emotions that demanded surrender, denounced all retaliations, and wore her defenses into the ground. What else could she do?

For this dynamic and gentle man she sprang the locks on her heart and allowed herself to give as effortlessly as she received.

Dan felt the change in her. He sensed a softening in her body, a freedom in her boldness, and was touched deeply by her tender generosity.

"Ah, Esther," he said with a groan, holding her tightly, his breath tickling her cheek as it came and went erratically. "You make me so crazy."

"Because I won't punch out Tommy Belldon's lights?"

"No. Just because of who you are and because I'm falling hopelessly in love with you all over again," he said lightly.

"Have I missed something?" she asked, confused by his statement, not sure of his seriousness by the tone of his voice.

"You've missed a lot, but I don't mind repeating myself."

"There's more to all this than you've told me, isn't there?"

"Yes. Lots more, but none of it is as bad as keeping and reading your diary," he said, not wanting her to think their life together was going to be a series of traumatic disclosures.

"Good. I don't think I could stand watching you make another confession," she said, pulling away to look into his dark, bottomless eyes.

"I can't believe you're not angry with me. I've felt like a heel from the first time I saw you in Bellewood."

"Well, I have to admit I'm not happy you found it or comfortable with the idea that you've read it, but things could have been a lot worse."

There it was again, he thought, proof that the proud, strong young woman in the diary still existed in her mature, sophisticated counterpart. The optimism that had refused to allow her to sink to the level of those around her had lifted her out of despair and kept her moving forward.

His next kiss was tender and adoring, long and consuming. It stroked the embers of their desire and warmed them with its extreme heat.

Esther never imagined she could feel like this. Dan was opening doors within her that even Seth hadn't been able to. Her love for her husband had been genuine and deep. With Seth's love she'd felt secure and appreciated for who she was. He had been her closest friend, a tender, caring lover, father of their long-awaited child. He'd shared a mutual need with her to make something of the life they'd been given, and they'd done it together.

Still, there hadn't been the nervous, anticipatory thrills she got just thinking of Dan. Seth's hands couldn't ignite the same craving hunger she felt for Dan. Dan's lips made her heart soar and sent her mind free-floating into oblivion.

She moaned her pleasure on a sigh as Dan took her face in his hands and pressed quick, loving kisses to her lips.

"I want you more than anything else in the world, Esther." He paused.

"But . . ." she prompted him with a sinking heart.

"But there's a lot to be said between us yet. There are things we need to know about each other. When we make love, I want it to be honest and open and everything between us to be the same way. When we make love, it'll be special, and there will be no turning back after that . . . for either of us."

Esther was amazed by his impassioned words. It had all seemed simple to her. They cared for each other, the attraction between them was staggering, they were both unencumbered by other relationships. . . .

"Maybe . . . maybe we should talk now," Esther said, moving out of his embrace.

She felt torn between her desire and the thought of ultimately hurting him if she weren't completely truthful now.

"I'm not going to try to deny how much I want to be with you, Dan." She laughed self-consciously. "You may have noticed how I've been throwing myself at you. I think you are incredibly kind and sensitive and sometimes you're almost funny in a dry sort of way, and I know we haven't known each other very long, but—"

"Esther, this isn't necessary."

"Yes, it is. I want you to understand," she said as a strange sort of panic rose within her. She suddenly realized that aside from Addy Markham, this man, this virtual stranger, was the only other person in the world she felt close to—the only one she trusted and felt she could count on. In all her life there had been only two others she'd held so dear to her, and they'd both died over a year ago.

Esther took a deep breath and started again.

"I'm not a person who puts a lot of stock in fairy tales, Dan. I don't believe in happily-ever-after—especially in relationships. I take my happiness when I can, where

I can. I never give out guarantees because I've never gotten any."

Dan moved toward her. He reached out and grasped her shoulders, then gently turned her to him.

"I understand, Esther," he said, locking his gaze with hers. "But that's how *you* feel, not how I do. I believe in dreams and wishes made on stars. I believe in people. I have to or my whole life would be pointless. I also happen to believe, very much, in you. Now I realize you're trying to protect me by warning me that we may not have any kind of future together, and I appreciate it, but it isn't necessary. You're wasting your breath on me, Esther. I believe there are some great things in store for us. You're just not ready to accept them yet."

"Dan, please. Please don't do this. I don't want you deluding yourself into thinking in terms of a permanent relationship. You deserve so much more than I'm capable of giving," Esther said sadly.

"Now who's deluding herself?"

A slow, knowing smile curled Dan's lips. He shook his head once as if in wonder, then kissed Esther in such a way as to melt every bone in her body.

"You keep throwing yourself at me," Dan murmured against her lips. "I don't mind at all and I'll always be there to catch you. But tonight I want you to think about what I've said."

Esther did think. Almost all night while her body ached and throbbed and she longed to be wrapped in his arms again, to feel his kiss again, to satisfy her hunger for him.

"What the hell does he want from me?" she finally asked herself in frustration. "Love?" The word left a nasty, metallic taste in her mouth. Did he want the kind of love her parents had for each other? The kind Addy Markham used to give if her partner had the price? The kind of love brothers have for sisters, or vice versa? The kind of love a mother has for her daughter that seems more like dutiful tolerance? The love neighbors have for fatherless children? The love between colleagues that was strong in good times and nonexistent in times of tragedy and despair? Those were the kinds of love she knew best.

Esther rolled over and over in bed, cursing Dr. Dogood and his beliefs. She was willing to give all she could. Trust and friendship were all Seth had ever asked of her, and he'd been her husband. Why couldn't Dan accept the same?

Did he want her to lie and promise him a tomorrow that might never come? Why couldn't he seize the moment and enjoy it?

Five

At breakfast there was no mention of what had transpired between them the previous night. Dan was friendly and easygoing, and acted as if nothing had happened, as if he weren't aware that his slightest glance sent tingles racing up and down Esther's spine, as if he were willing to give her all the time in the world to come to her senses, as if . . . as if his need for her weren't as great as her need for him. Could she be the only one feeling agonizing turmoil from within?—this madness that seemed to be taking possession not only of her body but her mind as well?

"What would you say to driving into D.C. on my next day off?" Dan asked brightly.

"What for?" Esther said disjointedly, her thoughts elsewhere.

"Fun?" His tone was dubious.

"Okay."

"Don't get too excited, it was only a suggestion. I have to go in on business, but that won't take more than five or ten minutes. If you think the trip will be too tiring—"

"No. No, I'd like to go. I'm just a little out of it this morning," she told him.

Dan's smile grew and his eyes took on a keenness that Esther was beginning to dread. It was as if he were reading her thoughts, and taking into consideration that he already knew most of her deepest secrets; her thoughts probably read as easily as a first-grade primer.

He didn't, however, read them aloud. He merely grinned at her, then pushed himself away from the breakfast table and prepared to leave for the clinic.

"Rest up today. We can discuss the trip later," he said as he passed her chair.

Esther heard him take three or four more steps and then stop. He retraced his way until he was beside her. He gathered her long dark hair in his hands and pulled it to one side, exposing her throat. She almost slid out of her chair when he kissed the curve of her neck in several different places and murmured, "Sleep at night. Think by day. I want you healthy and strong when we make love."

Esther was finishing washing the breakfast dishes when she heard the roar of a motorcycle on the access road leading to the mines. The driver turned onto the short dirt road in front of the house and stopped in the front yard. Young Eddy Belldon had come to visit, she thought.

Instead of coming to the door, the boy made himself comfortable on the front steps and waited. Esther wasn't sure how long his visit would last, so rather than risk Dan's anger, she slipped into her new thick down jacket and went out to face . . . her nephew.

The realization that Eddy was her nephew created an odd sensation in her. Never having had any relatives aside from her mother and Addy, who wasn't a blood relative, and the older Belldons, who didn't really count at all, it seemed strange that this young man should, in fact anyway, be her nephew.

"Hi," she said in greeting as she stepped out into the cold March air. "What brings you here?"

"Hi," he responded with a smile that was a lot less cocky than the one he'd given her the day before. "Is it okay for me to come here?" he asked bluntly.

"It's okay with me," Esther said with a shrug, "but your folks may not like it."

Ed Belldon nodded his awareness of that fact. "You shoulda heard all the screaming and yelling at our house last night. They sure don't like you much," he informed her, not seeming to care about his parents' quarrel or how they felt about Esther.

"I'd rather not hear about it, Eddy," she told him with a laugh. "As for their not liking me, well, the three of us never were very friendly."

"You sure are famous," he noted, changing the subject.

"I guess so." Esther sat on the steps next to him, wondering again what had brought him there.

"It must have been hard in the beginning, huh?" he commented as if he'd given it some thought.

"Yes, it was hard. But I was very lucky too."

"What made you decide to pick up and leave?" Ed asked, obviously ignorant about Esther's and his father's past.

"Lots of things," Esther said thoughtfully. "But I guess the strongest one was a decision I made long before I left. A decision I think everyone makes at some point in their life."

"Like what?" he asked, his attention riveted on Esther.

"Basically everyone has to make up their minds whether they're going to live a life similar to their parents or break away, take a different road and live a totally different sort of life. My choice was to be different," she explained quietly, knowing she should feel strange talking to Tom Belldon's son but feeling very at ease with him.

"You mean I can either be a miner like my dad or I can do something different, not be like him at all?" he asked, giving the subject some consideration.

"It's your life, not his," Esther pointed out.

They were silent for several minutes. The wind blew through the bare tree branches, making them creak and groan. The ever-present humming from the mines could be heard but was easy to ignore.

For the first time in days, Jasper the tabby cat had made another appearance, Esther noted absently. Apparently feeling antisocial, he sat on the porch rail on the far end of the house watching but not approaching.

"Was Seth Tobin as neat as he seemed?" Ed asked.

"Yes. He was a truly nice person," she said, her voice soft and wistful.

"I'm really sorry for you that he died," Ed said awkwardly. "Your baby too."

"Thank you," Esther said smoothly, deciding she liked this boy no matter who his father was. He was at a troubled age. He was too young to be an adult, too old to be a child. He was thoughtful and sensitive, and Esther had the distinct feeling that the black leather jacket and the big motorcycle helped him hide these two very vulnerable qualities.

Still ill at ease, the young man looked around vaguely. "I gotta go, but I want to come back. Is that okay?"

"Sure." She grinned. "Unless your parents forbid it. Neither one of us needs that kind of trouble. I don't want you or Dr. Jacobey getting mixed up in my problems, okay?"

"Okay," he agreed as he walked to his bike. "Although I don't know why they're making such a big deal of it. You seem okay to me."

Esther laughed. "Thank you, You're not so bad yourself."

He grinned at her, then slid the black helmet over his face and was soon gone. His quick, to-the-point visit was over, leaving Esther time to contemplate the

wonders of nature and how Tom and Jewel Belldon
ended up with such a nice son.

The hours between Eddy's visit and lunch were long
and nerve-racking for Esther. Invalidism wasn't a condition her mind or body took kindly to. She grew bored
and then restless as questions she didn't want to answer or that had no answers plagued her. The minute
hand on the clock seemed to take years to travel full
circle as she waited for Dan to come home. Even Addy,
who from years of habit was a night owl and preferred
to sleep late into the day, wouldn't make an appearance for at least another hour.

With nothing constructive to do, no one around to
entertain her, and with too much energy stored up to
sit and twiddle her thumbs, Esther was left with no
alternative but to seek distraction outside the familiar
walls of her childhood house.

The thick down jacket she'd purchased the day before was only minimal protection against the chill of
the brisk March winds. The cold was like a slap in the
face, clearing her mind and sharpening her senses. It
was just what she needed, Esther decided, as she stood
on the front porch taking in the muted winter colors in
the landscape around her.

Winters had always seemed to last so long when she
was young. She remembered the clear, bright skies
and bitter cold. As she walked along the access road,
she recalled how depressing she had always thought
the dead grass and lifeless trees were. How many times
had she had that exact same thought as she'd trudged
up and down the access lane to and from her bus stop
on the main road, she wondered.

In her mind's eye the trek had been much longer.
Then again, in those days her legs had been shorter
and Bellewood was as big as anything ever got. She'd
grown three inches and seen the world since the last

time she'd walked down this road. Yet it seemed like only yesterday.

It was easy to recall the feelings of anger she'd brought back from town when someone had taunted her. There were times when she'd dreaded coming home to her quiet, distracted mother and the gloomy house where Laura nurtured her shame. Lots of times she had wanted to keep on walking, past the mines, over the mountain, and away from Bellewood and the life she knew. She'd used the time it took to walk the distance to daydream about the life she'd make for herself someday. She would practice being gracious in her fame, charitable to those less fortunate and . . .

Wrapped up in her recollections, Esther didn't hear or see the finely tuned black car until it was nearly upon her. Obviously heading back to town from the mines, Tom Belldon's car slowed, then pulled to the side of the road.

Esther fought the panic that rose swiftly within her. The feeling of déjà vu weakened her knees. The last time she'd been alone on this road with Tom Belldon, he'd tried to rape her. The last time they'd been alone on this road was seventeen years ago, she reminded herself. Tom Belldon held less power over her now than he did then. Even as her heart faltered with fear and misgivings, her mind encouraged her to be bold and dauntless.

With great deliberation Esther matched his cold stare as Tom sat watching her from his car. When he made no move to confront her, she shrugged carelessly and went on with her walk, refusing to admit she felt almost giddy with relief.

"Esther!"

Esther stopped dead in her tracks, then slowly turned to face him.

"I meant what I said yesterday," he called. "I don't want you in my town. You've never caused anything but trouble around here and I won't tolerate it."

"Drop dead," she said. Not wishing to repeat yesterday's conversation, she headed toward the main road.

"Why'd you come back after all this time?" she heard him ask. It was a rash question—one she knew he hadn't meant to ask but didn't seem to have any control over.

Once again she turned to Tom Belldon.

"You can relax, Tom. It has nothing to do with you. I came back for purely personal reasons."

He got out of the car, advancing to within several feet of where she stood.

"That makes sense," he said. "Without Seth Tobin to hide behind, you'll be wanting to reevaluate your past, to decide whether or not it's acceptable for public scrutiny. I'd wondered when the truth about the poor little girl from West Virginia would come out."

Esther gave a short laugh and shook her head in disbelief. "Don't you ever let go of anything? You have more to hide in your past than I do. Being fatherless sort of pales in comparison to being a rapist, don't you think?"

The lines of Tom's face grew hard and defined. His eyes flashed dangerously at her implied threat, but Esther boldly pushed on.

"Tell you what, Tom. I'll make a deal with you. You stay out of my way while I'm in Bellewood and leave Addy and the doctor alone, and your little indiscretion can remain a secret between us. But I have to warn you. I'm not someone you should feel free to kick around anymore. I'm famous and rich. I'll tear you to shreds if I have to."

Esther's words sounded tough to her own ears. It was gratifying to her, because she knew that her cockiness was just an act.

"You always were a big talker who didn't know her place, Esther."

"Try me, Tom. I'm not the girl I once was."

"I'm sure that's debatable, but we'll see. You do what

you have to, then get yourself out of my town, Esther. And I warn you, if you so much as look cross-eyed while you're here, I'll come down on you so fast you won't know what hit you."

"I'm not a convict. When you get right down to it, there isn't a whole lot of bite to your bark, Tom."

"I'm not a kid anymore either, Esther. Don't underestimate me."

"Okay. We'll call it a standoff this time. You leave me alone, and I won't make waves while I'm here. Deal?"

Tom didn't answer. He gave her one last considering look and turned back to his car. He didn't bother to glance her way when he drove past—that would have given their discussion a certain degree of importance. Esther made a derisive snort. She and her brother had certainly gotten their fair share of pride and bravado.

Prudently Esther decided to keep her meeting with Tom Belldon to herself. There was no telling how Dan would react if he learned that she had not only failed to take a swing at her brother once again, but had instead struck a bargain with him.

Esther couldn't help the smile or the warm feeling she had recalling Dan's protectiveness.

The next few days passed uneventfully, much to Esther's dismay. Although Dan, unfortunately for Esther, began to display a latent musical talent as he skillfully played her like a finely tuned Stradivarius.

She would feel his presence in a room and look up to find him watching her and immediately her heart would begin to race painfully in her chest. He seemed incapable of coming within ten feet of her without touching her in some way. The brush of his hand across her back as she sat at the table sent sparks flying inside her, tensing her body with anticipation. His hands on her shoulders as he interfered in her game of solitaire filled her with a lingering hope and eagerness that remained long after Dan had moved away.

However, Esther hadn't been a prostitute's daughter, hadn't been raised in the shadow of a madam or been married without learning a little bit about the male of the species. She knew that Dan wanted her. He'd told her as much. Perhaps not to the same degree as she wanted him, but she felt certain the need and desire were there. She finally felt she had no recourse but to fight back in the only way she could think of. She unleashed the impelling forces that tempted her and took every opportunity to obtain what satisfaction she could.

When Dan's arm encircled her waist, his hand resting comfortably on her hip as he bent to smell their dinner cooking on the stove, Esther turned into him, wrapping her arms around him, hoping desperately he'd complete the embrace. He did so in the most natural, unassuming way, as if holding her in his arms were as easy for him as breathing. And yet as he stroked her hair and rocked her slowly from side to side, he conveyed to Esther the feeling that holding her was not only as easy for him as breathing, but it was just as vital.

Emboldened by Dan's cooperation, Esther fearlessly forged ahead. After she insinuated herself in Dan's arms as they watched television late one evening, she waited for her body to tell her when his gaze was upon her. In that moment she looked up, her intentions and desires clear. Dan merely smiled and lowered his lips to hers in compliance.

Esther's taut nerves and muscles went instantly limp as she wallowed in the sensations Dan created with his lips, teeth, and tongue. Full of passion and promises, each kiss felt as if it would be their last. His hands roamed over her possessively, as if he'd covered this territory a thousand times and knew all its best and most favorite places.

He kissed her long and deeply, drawing out her life's breath, replacing it with his until she was filled with a desperate urgency to share more of herself, to give herself totally to Dan and become one with him. And then his kisses slowed, became gentle and tender, soothing Esther into a state of mindless lassitude.

"You should go to sleep soon if you intend to get up early and drive into D.C. with me in the morning," Dan said, his voice thicker and deeper than Esther had ever heard it before.

She looked into his eyes expecting to see a teasing twinkle, but found none. He was serious. Feeling confused and rejected even as his fingers caressed her cheek in a loving way, Esther's mind went blank. She couldn't think of anything to say. After all, she had her pride. Esther could only do so much advancing. There was a halfway point to everything, and she'd already crossed over it.

"I guess so," she replied, trying to hide the hurt and disappointment in her voice as she started to move away.

"Esther," Dan said, pulling her close once again, "our time will come. I promise you. And if it makes you feel any better, this is very hard on me too. I've made love to you in my head a thousand different ways, and my body is so eager to share them with you, it's about to explode. But there's a lot about me that you don't know. Don't you *want* to know more about me? Remember, I told you that once we make love, there'll be no turning back."

"Well, short of your being a homicidal maniac, couldn't we just get to know each other as we go?"

"No," he said, his voice gentle but firm. "There's a lot at stake here . . . for me anyway, and although people are constantly changing and learning about each other in a relationship, I think you and I at least should know who the other is now, at this moment."

Misunderstanding, Esther was hurt again by his words.

"You're so right, Doctor. A man can't go to bed with

the bastard child of a whore and not wonder what he's gotten himself into," Esther said angrily as she pushed on his chest to free herself, her eyes clouding with tears.

"I'm not referring to you, Esther," Dan said as he struggled to keep her near him. "I mean me. Most of your life has been an open book to me, including your diary. I know who you are, what you are, what you're capable of. But you don't know a damned thing about me."

"I know you're kind and gentle and understanding. I know I trust you, and that's a hell of a lot more than I've ever bothered to find out about most of the people I've met," she said, still distraught.

"I know, my sweet Esther Brite. You would have moved in with Addy two weeks ago if you hadn't found something in me you wanted or needed. You see," he said cajolingly. "I do know you very well. Just give us a little more time so that you can know me as well."

Reluctantly Esther agreed, though her mind went a-dither with questions. What on earth wasn't he telling her about himself? What could be so bad that he couldn't just say it? Lord knew he wasn't a shy man when it came to saying things he thought needed to be said. So what was he hiding? What else was there to know about him, she wondered.

The trip into Washington D.C., began shortly after the sun came up. The day was bright and clear, but the wind remained bitterly cold. The sunshine had been unable to melt the heavy snowfall from several days earlier because of the low temperatures. The winter chill settled in Esther's bones and made her shiver while she waited impatiently for the Bronco's heating system to kick in and warm her.

Dan's nose and cheeks were bitten pink by the wind as he climbed in after scraping the frost off the windshield.

"Damn, it's cold," he muttered, rubbing his hands together.

"Ever considered living in California?" Esther asked.

"Never. What would I have to complain about there?"

"The rain."

"I love it when it rains. Especially in the spring, when it smells so sweet and fresh and turns the world green again. It's like life starting all over, giving everyone another chance," Dan said, putting the Bronco in motion.

"At what?" Esther asked.

"At everything—new life, new loves, new goals."

"And what happens when winter comes again? How do you feel then?"

"It depends. If I've had a good year, I have my happiness to keep me warm all winter. If things didn't work out for me, I wait the winter out and try again in the spring," Dan told her, flashing a quick grin in her direction.

"You handle success and failure that easily?"

"Actually, no," he said. "I just thought that would sound very philosophical. In truth, I handle it like most people . . . maybe worse. I don't take kindly to failure."

"Who does?" Esther questioned more to herself than Dan.

Failure. The word had a cold, clear, alarming sound to it. It scared her. It was something she'd never tolerated in her life.

"Look," Dan said, breaking the silence between them. "If I were making this trip alone, which I usually do, I'd do it all in one day. But it's almost five hours one way. You'll be tired. Why don't we stay over and drive back early tomorrow."

"Oh, no. Not on my account. I can sleep in the car on the way back if I get too tired. Please don't change your plans because of me."

"Actually, it would be because of you, but my motives

are purely selfish. It's been a . . . while since the opportunity to take a beautiful woman to dinner has presented itself."

"Thank you," said Esther, still remarkably uncomfortable with his calling her beautiful. "But I'm not really dressed for the occasion."

Dan glanced at her wool slacks and thick down jacket. He looked at the road and then back at Esther. "In a gunnysack you'd put most women to shame, Esther. But if you'd feel better dressed up, that can be arranged too." He was pensive for a moment, then continued. "And we'll stay with my uncle. He'll be ecstatic," he said in a weary voice.

"Don't you like your uncle?" she asked in response to his tone.

"I love him. But at the moment we're having a difference of opinion. Hopefully with you there he won't try to press his point too hard."

Mile after mile of barren winter countryside passed by while Esther and Dan talked happily in the now warm and cozy Bronco.

Esther had traveled this road only twice before in her life. The first time she'd been numb with anger and despair. The second time, just a little over a month ago, she had been dazed with fever. This time she was happy and content and excited, alert to the green, brown, and yellow of the landscape as it leveled out to form hills and dales for as far as she could see.

She poured coffee from a thermos for Dan and handed him doughnuts from a box while he told her about his parents and younger sister and what growing up in a small town in Virginia had been like. He spoke with pride about coming from a long line of doctors on both sides of his family. And yet, for just an instant, Esther sensed a sadness in him that seemed to come and go so quickly, she thought maybe she'd imagined it.

He went on to describe his uncle, whom they were going to stay with. A doctor himself, he had taken Dan under his wing as a medical student and had been a tremendous help during Dan's internship and residency. Dan confided that he also had a hunch his uncle had used his considerable influence on the hospital's board of directors when they were looking for a qualified physician to head the shock-trauma unit.

"It was a dream come true for me," Dan said. "In those days trauma centers were just beginning to be recognized as necessities. We used to waste so much valuable time in the emergency room calling in doctors, gathering an OR crew . . . even getting the patient to the hospital quickly and efficiently was a problem. Now, instead of hours, we can treat trauma victims in a matter of minutes and not a second is wasted," he said proudly.

"And you were bored to death with all of that and decided to move to Bellewood, where even coherent conversation would be a real challenge to you," Esther said facetiously.

Dan grinned, but he was very sincere when he replied. "Actually, I loved it. I ate it, slept it, breathed it, but . . . for too long. There was nothing else in my life. I didn't want anything else. After a while I wasn't running the unit, it was running me. And the more I gave, the more it wanted."

"And moving to Bellewood was supposed to break the cycle?"

Dan nodded. "I considered it only a temporary position, but once I got there, I found I was in a lot worse shape than I had imagined. I'd stopped treating people as people. They had become cases without faces, meat on a slab. I . . . hated who I had become," he said, shame heavy in his voice.

There was silence between them as Esther searched for a way to comfort him.

"Well, you've obviously recovered. I know Addy firmly believes that you walk on water. And she wouldn't be so completely convinced if you weren't a compassionate man."

"What do *you* think, Esther? Do you think I could walk on water?" Dan asked.

Dan slowed the Bronco to a stop and was preparing to make a left-hand turn off the highway into a small roadside inn. He looked over at Esther, eager for her answer.

She couldn't suppress the snort of laughter that bubbled up in her. "Hardly," she replied honestly. "In fact, when we first met I thought you could probably freeze water with your eyes, but even then I could feel a great gentleness and caring in you. And now that you've warmed up to me a little, I know you to be very kind and understanding . . . especially about all the stuff in my past."

"Does it bother you that I know the truth?"

Dan made the turn and pulled into a parking place close to the front door of the inn.

"To a certain degree," Esther said, busying herself with the seat belt, avoiding his gaze. When Dan looked at her, she always had the feeling that her thoughts were no longer hers alone.

There was a long silence before Dan spoke in a quiet voice.

"Would you like to know exactly what I think of you and your past? Would you be more comfortable knowing?"

"I'm not sure."

"To begin with, you weren't the first or the last illegitimate child to be born. Secondly, it wasn't your fault you *were* born, although I'm certainly glad it happened. And thirdly," he said, "I have never in my life admired or respected anyone more than I do that gutsy little girl in your diary. She's courageous and unconquerable. She's bright and witty and giving and I'm very much in love with her."

There it was, thought Esther grimly, her heart and mind racing in a panic of confusion and doubt. Love. It was exactly as she had suspected. He wouldn't have told her he loved her if he didn't want her to reply in kind.

Did trusting him, caring about him, and counting him among the too few people she considered her friends constitute love? Was the frantic attraction she felt toward him—wanting to please him, to make him happy—anything even remotely related to the phenomenon of love, or was it simply something similar to the feeling animals have when the need to mate and propagate consumes them?

Even the feeling of oneness she had with Dan, the feeling that they were somehow connected, didn't really live up to the magical, bell-ringing, catastrophic qualities love was supposed to possess. Rather, it was a warm, comfortable linking of spirits, a quiet welcoming, an intrinsic belonging.

But love? Could the way she felt about Dan be called love? The only time she'd ever truly known love for someone was the love she had for her baby. How could she possibly explain to Dan that she wasn't sure what passionate man-woman love was?

Dan hadn't meant to blurt out his feelings. The words simply had fallen from his lips in a most natural way, like they did in his dreams. Poor Esther looked ready to bolt and run. She wasn't ready to admit to the way she felt, but she would be . . . and soon.

They used the inn's facilities and drove across the street to gas up the Bronco. She was relieved that Dan seemed unaffected by her lack of response. If anything, he was making a great effort to help her relax again, and she appreciated it. She laughed at his college anecdotes and listened attentively to his thoughts on Bellewood.

Had she known that putting Dan in an automobile and turning the motor on would bring forth such a burst of talkativeness in him, she might have done it weeks before. It was almost as if he were bent on telling Esther as much about himself as he already knew about her.

If this was the case, Esther didn't mind. Like a sponge,

she soaked it all in, savoring the knowledge, thirsty for more. Besides, if telling her his life story brought him any closer to satisfying her need for him, then . . . well, maybe not. She'd be back to the questions of love and the future. Dan was going to ask for both eventually, she knew for certain. Perhaps talking would be best for the time being, she decided.

Esther's heart sank in confusion and despair. She only half listened to Dan, while in the back of her mind she pondered her quandary.

They arrived in Washington, D.C., shortly before noon, going first to the elegant old brownstone in Georgetown owned by Dan's Uncle Fesstus.

"The boy has no manners at all," Fesstus Jordon complained to Esther. "Not only does he not call to say he'll be dropping in, but he's never once mentioned he even knew you. And I'm a great fan of yours."

"Thank you, Dr. Jordon, but—"

"Fesstus. Please," he said.

"Thank you again, Fesstus, but I'm afraid it's my fault you didn't get any advance warning. You see—"

"No. No, now. Don't make excuses for him," the old man said. "He never calls. Just shows up expecting to be welcomed. This time he brought you for the shock effect. He's hoping I'll drop dead of a heart attack and leave him this house."

"That makes sense to me," Esther said. "It's a beautiful house."

Fesstus Alby Jordon, approaching seventy years old, was tall and lean like his nephew. Olive-skinned and dark-eyed as well, there was a youthfulness and exuberance about him. And unlike the sober, serious look that often clouded Dan's eyes, his uncle's shown with humor and wisdom.

The elderly gentleman was very proud of his home, boasting that he bought it from a crooked politician thirty years previous. He gave Esther the grand tour while Dan went to the rear of the house to greet his uncle's longtime housekeeper and arrange for coffee.

Aside from beautiful antique furnishings Fesstus showed Esther, he lingered, bragging over his collections. His two favorites seemed to be a group of old and unusual nutcrackers and an array of gruesome-looking medical instruments.

"Actually, some of them are quite ingenious when you consider what little they knew of medicine in those days. Take the scalpel, though, it's changed very little over the years. What does that tell you about modern medicine, hmm?" Fesstus wondered aloud.

"It tells you to hope that at least the men using it have changed," Dan said from the doorway.

Carrying a large ornate tea service, Dan entered the room. From out of nowhere Esther was awash with a feeling of gladness. She hadn't been aware that she'd been missing him.

"Ah," the older man said with great satisfaction as he took his seat in a large leather chair. "Am I to be, once again, lectured on the nonexistent omnipotence and omniscient powers of the modern surgeon? How delightful."

"Not today, Uncle," Dan said pointedly to Fesstus. "Sorry."

"What a shame. I'm sure Esther would be interested to know how that particular line of thinking is ruining the best set of hands I've seen in my life," Fesstus argued.

"Maybe. But not today," Dan insisted.

Esther was confused . . . and curious.

"No maybe about it, Dan. Look at her. She's very interested."

Dan's gaze met Esther's. Collected in the depths of his dark eyes she saw his struggle, his pain and sorrow. He seemed to reach out to her for comfort. She felt his emotions intensely, but was helpless.

Fesstus, seizing their silent communication as a prime time to drive home his point, said, "Dan is of the opinion, you see, that surgeons are not allowed to be human or make mistakes. They must be all-powerful, all-knowing, or they are totally useless."

The tension in the room was oppressive. The silence grew louder by the second. Esther could hear her own heart beating in her chest. She held her breath, afraid that even the slightest breeze would inflict more pain on Dan.

It was Dan, however, who finally broke the stillness. Apparently he'd found what he wanted to see in Esther's eyes, or he'd given up looking for it. His gaze lowered, went briefly to his uncle, and then to the tea service on the table.

Esther watched his stiff movements as he poured and passed her a cup of coffee. She remained silent while he repeated the gesture for his uncle. He sat back with his own cup and began to speak.

"Five years ago I was on duty when they brought in a fourteen-year-old girl. She was a young prostitute who had been taught a very good lesson by her own father. He had discovered what she was doing after school and had said that if she wanted to sell herself like a piece of cheap meat, her customers ought to get what they pay for." There was a brief silence before he could go on. "She looked like hamburger."

"I worked eight hours straight on her that night. She died after the first hour, and I just kept on sewing her up using little, tiny, fine sutures so she wouldn't have any scars. When I finished, I looked up to find I was the only one left in the OR. My patient was dead and I didn't even know her name. I walked out of there feeling totally useless, and it wasn't just because of the girl. I—I kept asking myself how something like that could happen. The thought of spending the rest of my life sewing up the atrocities that we humans inflict on one another was unbearable . . . so I kept on walking."

Nausea and an aching sympathy filled Esther. She sat holding her warm coffee cup, hands trembling, eyes clouding with tears, unable to utter a single word.

Fesstus was quiet even though his eyes held no great pity for Dan. Rather, Esther saw a tender understanding and wise empathy reflected in their depths, as well as a considerable amount of determination.

"I've had time to heal in Bellewood," Dan said. "I've realized that particular case was simply the last straw from a huge haystack. I enjoy medicine again. Most of the cases I treat now are the result of unavoidable accidents and diseases that no man has the power to prevent."

"And your talented hands?" Fesstus said. "Will you let your gift atrophy because you can't pick and choose the types of suffering they can relieve?"

Dan held up his long slim fingers and wiggled them energetically while he said, "I give 'em a workout every once in a while. A baby here, a bone there. Every so often I work on a gallbladder or appendix. They're happy."

"Impossible," Fesstus said. "No one is happy if they're not living up to their potential."

"Well," Dan said, standing, "that remains to be seen in my case. In the meantime, I have an appointment."

Finally Dan turned back to Esther. With all her heart she wanted to say or do just the right thing to ease Dan's plight. It was infuriating to know so many words, to have expressed her thoughts and emotions so many times before and still be unable to put three simple words together.

He must have read her thoughts, because in that moment she received the most loving and understanding smile from him she'd ever seen.

"And you, my sickie, are to sleep," Dan said. "When I take a woman out on the town, I hate it if she's drooping all over the furniture."

The previous discussion apparently closed, and

Fesstus also apparently choosing to let it rest for the moment, effectively broke the tension in the room. Leaping at the chance to lighten Dan's mood, Esther said, "Let's make a deal. Let me go shopping and I'll eat lots of starch at dinner."

Dan stared at her for several seconds.

"If I eat starch, I won't droop. Get it?" she said helpfully, already beginning to feel a little foolish.

Dan grimaced. "I knew this trip was going to be too much for you. Go on up to sleep and we'll worry about your clothes later."

Esther noted he was hard-pressed to keep his grin under control as he moved toward her. Extending one hand, he helped her to stand. As always when he was within smelling distance, Esther's heartrate sped up a little and her muscles began to tingle with excitement.

The reaction was well founded this time as Dan cupped her face in his hands and pressed a tender, earth-shaking kiss to her lips.

"Sleep," he ordered in a firm whisper against her lips. He kissed her once more and left.

Fesstus was Mr. Congeniality once again as he showed Esther to her room. She had resented his harsh, cruel words to Dan earlier, but she instinctively felt he had meant well. Like Addy Markham, Fesstus Jordon was evidently a man who believed a sharp stab was less painful than a jagged cut when it came to the people he cared about. The fact that he loved Dan was obvious in his expression and in the way he told Esther, "You're good for him. He's never told me exactly what happened that night and I've given him plenty of opportunities. He talked about it today only so that you would understand. He wanted you to know. I . . . I'm grateful that he has you to confide in, Esther."

Six

Esther woke in a cherrywood four-poster. The wallpaper was a federal-blue print, the drapes were thick, heavy, and drawn. Nothing looked familiar, and it took several seconds before she could orient herself.

Having slept deeply, she felt dazed, a drugged feeling that she wallowed in for several minutes before she recalled her date with Dan—and her clothes, or lack thereof.

She was out of bed and halfway to the door before she spotted the boxes piled neatly in a wing chair near the window. There was a card carefully folded and propped on top.

> While you slept I had a most interesting and pleasurable afternoon. Fesstus got us tickets for the musical at the Kennedy Center. Your being there will keep me from sneaking out in the middle of it. You, in this, will definitely keep me awake. Come down when you're ready.
>
> Love,
> Dan

Seth had always enjoyed buying Esther jewelry, lovely pieces of art, and the latest in modern conveniences or extravagances. Never had anyone bought her something as intimate as a cream-colored silk teddy or anything as beautiful as the Chinese-blue gown Dan had chosen. Of a lustrous silk, the flared skirt fell from a fitted empire waist while a lace flounce and stand-up collar covered her shoulders, creating a graceful, elegant capelet effect. The soft folds molded and clung to Esther's tall, slim frame. It swished when she walked, and she'd never felt more beautiful.

Bathed and powdered, her hair wound loosely atop her head, Esther left the room. Dan must have been listening for her, because as she came to the top of the stairs he emerged from the library on the first floor and looked up in her direction.

The expression on Dan's face mirrored her own emotions. Dressed in dark formal wear, Dan was without a doubt the most handsome man she'd ever seen. Esther's heart began to flutter and her breath caught in her throat. Dan's tall form and broad shoulders seemed even taller and broader in black, and Esther suddenly felt small and vulnerable by comparison. But it was his eyes that affected her most. Dark and intense, they took possession of her. Her skin grew warm and burned as he branded her with his gaze, bonding her to him for all time.

Oddly enough Esther accepted Dan's fetters without reservation, welcoming them. Because in the split second of unspoken passion that passed between them, she realized that not only was he tying her to him, but he was requesting bondage to her as well. For all time he would be hers—not out of a sense of duty or friendship, not because it would be easy or convenient or because of some fluke of fate. He was hers because he wanted to be and in his wanting was his love—the key Esther had been searching for.

Dan took several steps toward her as she began to descend the stairs.

"You are so beautiful," he uttered quietly as if afraid to break the spell.

"Thank you," Esther said, allowing her gaze to say so much more than she ever could with words.

The night was like a fairy-tale dream. Vaguely she would remember the small, elegant restaurant where they'd dined. She would recall dancing in Dan's arms to music only they could hear. She wouldn't remember what she ate, if she ate at all. And vividly she would relive walking the historic streets of Washington, D.C., arm in arm with Dan, their inability to converse on the mundane, the difficult silences, and the long, yearning glances.

She would cherish the kisses they exchanged in the cab and wonder what the name of the musical was that they saw at the Kennedy Center. Her guess was the play had something to do with sailors. What she knew for a fact was that an unaccustomed sense of peace and belonging had settled around her heart as she sat holding Dan's hand.

Every minute was a whirl of excitement and sensations for her, the source of which was Dan. Every glance, every word, the merest touch from him was a caress to Esther. She was heady on love, amazed at how simple it seemed and how alive and complex it was at the same time.

It wasn't enough just to crave someone physically. She'd known that long ago. Nor was it enough to simply respect, admire, and care about someone. It was a mixture of the two and so much more that Esther was feeling as she turned to Dan at her bedroom door.

"I told you before I couldn't offer you any guarantees," Esther said. "I still can't, but I want to. More than anything, I'd like to tell you everything between us will stay as perfect as it is this moment, but I can't.

All I can tell you is that if I could make such a promise, I'd make it to you."

"Why?" Dan asked, his muscles tense, his heart yearning to hear the words his dreams were made of.

"Because I . . . I love you. You've become so important to me. I want so much to spend every second we have together making you feel as safe and cherished and as uniquely special as you make me feel. Whether the time for us lasts only through the night or for the next two hundred years, I want to spend it with you."

Dan placed one hand near the nape of her neck and the other at her waist to draw her close. Esther could feel his heart beating in cadence with her own, could feel his ragged breathing against her chest, and was surprised to feel him tremble as he held her.

"Was it so hard for you to admit it?" he asked, stroking her cheek gently with the pad of his thumb.

"No. I've felt this way for a while, but I didn't know what it meant. It's . . . not something I've had much experience with."

"That's not true, Esther. You have an infinite capacity for loving. I've heard it in your music, read it in your diary, seen it in your eyes. It's your love and faith in mankind that's kept all your heartaches from turning you into a bitter, vengeful woman. You just have a little trouble accepting love from others. You've been hurt so often, you've learned to protect yourself by not expecting people to love you. When they do, you don't believe them or you think it's a trick."

Esther was thoughtful, recalling the few people she'd trusted and how most of them had failed her. She may not have cut herself off consciously, but she'd had every right to, she decided.

"Things happen and people make mistakes, Esther," Dan said gravely.

Esther wasn't sure if it was the tone of his voice or the simplicity of his words that caused her to take a more serious look into the face of the man she loved.

She saw the same handsome face that had so intrigued her in the beginning, but now saw so much more through her loving eyes: The humor in the crow's feet that fanned out at the corners of his eyes, the lines of compassion, knowledge, and wisdom across his brow and around his mouth, his tender, sensuous nature in the curve of his lips, his trustworthiness. And yet there was an uncertainty in his words that she could feel as strongly as she felt his love.

"I can't make you any guarantees either, Esther. I can't promise I'll never hurt you or that you won't find yourself alone again someday. I don't know what will happen tomorrow any more than you do. All I know is that I love you more than anyone or anything else in my life. And with that love comes a hope for the future, the desire to grow old with you, to share every second between now and then with you, making you happy and content," Dan said.

Esther could feel her breasts heaving with the emotion his words aroused in her. Never had her own music sounded as sweet or as impassioned as his words did now. Never had she felt so wanted or so close to anyone as she did to Dan.

In a sudden act born of frustration, Dan pushed Esther into her room, flipped the switch that lit the bedside lamps, and firmly closed the door behind him.

"Words aren't enough. They're inadequate and too easily misunderstood. I can't explain the way you fill me so completely. My mind, my body, my soul . . . whatever it is that keeps me alive, keeps me looking forward to living from one moment to the next, are all focused on you. I have this insane, almost animallike need to possess you, to take care of you and protect you. I—I'm actually crazy in love with you, Esther," Dan said with a half laugh.

Esther had the strange sensation that she was falling apart at the seams. Her arms hung heavily and without feeling at her sides. For all she knew, they might have fallen off. The passion and power Dan had expressed was numbing even though she knew her heart was racing wildly and something deep inside her was screaming for fewer words and more action.

"Show me," she said.

Into Dan's eyes came the animallike need he had spoken of earlier, and Esther knew fear and excitement at once. She almost screamed when his hands reached out for her, but they were the gentle, deft, and experienced hands of a man who knew what he wanted.

In a matter of seconds Esther stood naked before him. She shivered while Dan's gaze moved freely over her body. With the tips of his fingers he outlined her breasts as if fascinated by their smoothness and shape. Esther held her breath, afraid of disrupting the ripples of exquisite delight passing through her. He grazed one hard nipple with his thumb and her painfully engorged and throbbing breast seemed to swell and burn. Esther closed her eyes to ward off the dizziness that blurred her vision, and moaned softly.

She felt Dan's fingers curl under her chin and lift her face to his. She forced her eyes open and met his gaze. In his eyes she read the certainty that from that moment on she belonged to him alone. Never would she crave another man's body. Never again would her heart be free to seek out another. This was the moment he'd spoken of, the moment there was no turning away from. She grew faint as if he'd tapped into her very essence and made that his as well.

Esther reached out to Dan. Her fingers met warm, hard sinew. Vaguely she wondered where his clothes had gone, but the thought was instantly superfluous. Dan's hands covered hers on his chest and then he drew them up around his neck, encouraging her to be bold with him.

His hands slid down her arms and over her back to rest finally on her hips, leaving a scorching trail of heat in their wake. His eyes were mesmerizing as he gazed deep into hers.

"I love you, Esther Brite," he said simply, then drew her closer to show her the depth and scope of his passion.

Esther was awestruck. That anyone, especially this man, could love her with such fierceness and reverence was not only joyous, but humbling. She ached to be worthy, to show him in return the vastness of her own passion, to share with him her newly found secrets of love.

The hunger and thirst they had denied for so long consumed them quickly. They each fed on the other's needs, feasted on the acute excitement they created. They drank to intoxication the satisfaction and fulfillment they both sought until all too soon delirium overtook them, exploding deep within them, fusing them together for all time.

Dan moved to release Esther from his weight but she held on to him tightly, still shaken by the aftermath of their loving. "Don't leave me. Please, don't leave me," she pleaded.

Moving up on his elbows, Dan took Esther's face in his hands, forcing her to look at him while he said, "I can't leave you, Esther. Even if I wanted to, I couldn't. You are too much a part of my life. Our bond goes far beyond this life and into the next. And it goes both ways, you know," he said, and grinned at her lovingly. "If you ever try to leave me, I'll track you down and force you to come back."

"Force?" Esther asked with raised brows. He was smiling and his tone was light, but she wasn't at all sure he was kidding.

"Force," he repeated with an affirmative nod of his head. "I wasn't paying much attention last time, but this time I plan to discover your every weakness." He bent his head to nuzzle her neck as he continued. "In very short order I plan to know your body better than I know my own. I'll make you a slave to my loving. And if you ever try to leave me, all I'll have to do is whisper what I'd do to you in your ear . . . like this . . . and you'll beat me home to bed."

"My goodness," Esther said in mock astonishment. "For such a quiet, reserved man, I never dreamed you'd be so cocky in bed."

"Fesstus says there's a distinct difference between cocky and confident surgeons. I claim the same distinction here."

"My, my," she said teasingly as she thrilled to the feel of him growing inside her, happier and more content than she could ever remember being. "Well, what happens if I play the stoic and keep my weaknesses to myself?"

Dan's eyes shone with an evil wickedness as he drew his hand away from her face and moved it slowly down her body.

"Esther. Esther. Don't even try it. I didn't go to med school just to become a doctor, you know."

This time there was no frantic fury in Dan to possess her. Esther was one vulnerable nerve ending, a total weakness to his every kiss, nibble, and touch. She accepted his adoration and cherished it. In return she loved him with her whole heart and soul.

He was right. Dan was part of her now. Every fiber of her being embraced him as if it were the most natural thing in the world for her to do. Esther was amazed again at how easy it was to love, to give of herself, and receive in kind.

Slowly, Dan memorized her body, then taught her to respond to every nuance of his touch. He led her to a state of bliss she'd never before visited. They frolicked and played until the sun began to glow in the east. Then they slept, oblivious to every thing except each other and the feelings they shared.

The next morning Esther awoke with a smile on her lips. She was alone in bed, but that didn't dampen her spirits. She could feel Dan's impression in the sheets beside her, smell him on the pillow near hers. His words of love still resounded in her ears, and she didn't have to close her eyes to conjure up the feel of his arms around her.

The smile remained as she showered and dressed. She knew she must look a fool, grinning inanely, eyes glazed—but she didn't care. Fesstus could think what he liked and undoubtedly his assumptions would be right. She couldn't bring herself to repress the grin or the sparkle in her eyes or the lightness in her steps as she emerged from her room and started for the main floor.

"Sullivan is resigning in two months," Esther heard Fesstus say in an angry voice from the library as she stood at the foot of the stairs. "Now is your chance to come back and pick up where you left off. You're wasting your life, not to mention your talent in that godforsaken little mining town. This is where you're needed, Dan." There was a brief pause and a calmer Fesstus continued. "If it's the directors you're worried about, I've already sent out a few feelers and—"

"Is that what all the brouhaha was about yesterday?" Dan asked, his voice weary and aggravated.

"You went to the board yesterday?"

"I was summoned. I thought I'd gotten involved in a lawsuit or something. If I'd known what you were up to, I'd have saved the gas."

"What happened? What did they say?"

"Nothing," Dan replied testily.

"Dan." Fesstus's voice was as cold as ice. "What did you tell them?"

Dan forced Fesstus—and Esther—to wait for his answer. When he spoke, his voice was quiet and controlled. It wasn't hard for Esther to imagine the look on his face.

"They wanted to know how I was and what kind of plans I had for the future. I told them I was terrific and that I was planning to marry a beautiful woman, if she'll have me, have a million babies with her, and live happily ever after," Dan said rather matter-of-factly.

"And the position of chief surgeon in the trauma unit?" Fesstus asked.

"I told 'em I'd think about it, but," he said pointedly, "don't get your hopes up."

"Well, it's more than you'd concede to three years ago," Fesstus said optimistically.

"Fess. Please. Stay out of it. This is my life—mine and Esther's. We'll decide."

Esther remained at the bottom of the staircase, shamelessly listening in with mixed emotions. Part of her was elated at hearing his plans for their future . . . part of her wasn't. That part was resentful that he'd say anything to Fesstus before he'd said anything definite to her about marriage and children. It seemed rather presumptuous of him. Not necessarily in contrast to her own wishes, but presumptuous nonetheless. Then, too, there was her inclusion in his ultimate decision. It shouldn't matter what she thought. Hell, she couldn't even control her own life. How could she possibly advise Dan about his? Which brought Esther to the most important question: How *could* she help him? She understood his fears, his feelings of inadequacy, his hesitancy to take that first step. But understanding wasn't always enough.

"Dan? Fesstus? Anyone home?" she called, giving them the choice to either close or continue their discussion before she made an appearance.

Dan joined her instantly. From the look on his face she would never have guessed at the conversation she had just interrupted. Dan was all smiles, as she herself had been moments before. His eyes twinkled with the knowledge of a night no other human knew of, save the two of them. Every whispered word, every touch and moan of ecstasy was silently replayed between them as they stood grinning happily at each other.

"Morning," Dan finally said, his voice huskier than usual.

"Hi," Esther returned on a sigh of delight.

She came eye to eye with him, and her body quickened with the anticipation of his touch as she placed her hands on his shoulders.

"Sleep well?" she asked innocently.

"Never better," Dan said as his hands splayed to encompass her waist and draw her closer. Their kiss was an abridged version of those they'd shared the night before, full of love and promises.

"Georgia has your breakfast ready," he said, his voice a near caress. "We can leave after you eat."

"I'm not really hungry for food."

"No eatie, no treatie," Dan said humorously. "I like my women strong and healthy."

"Yes, master," Esther said teasingly in return.

Both Dan and Fesstus joined Esther for coffee while she ate. The conversation was, of necessity, kept light. They avoided the subject of Dan's work so as not to reignite Fesstus and any matter that could conceivably cause Esther and Dan to leap away from the table and attack the other in a fit of mad passion.

"Did you happen to notice how often the national debt was brought up in that . . . conversation," Dan asked a short while later as he maneuvered their way out of the city and back onto the interstate.

"My count was four times, but I have to admit I was a bit distracted," Esther said.

"So was your foot. It got lost up the leg of my pants."

"Is that why you were squirming so uncomfortably?"

Dan shot her a quailing look but turned away quickly as he began to laugh.

"You deserved it," Esther said in defense of her actions. "All that garbage about indentured servants and harem girls was getting on my nerves."

• • • •

And so they passed the hours in close confabulation. It was as if the length of their acquaintance could be measured in years or lifetimes rather than in mere days.

At midday they stopped at a grocery store in a small town in Maryland and bought supplies for their lunch. Esther stood pondering a rack of candy bars while Dan paid for the more nutritional food. When they finished, Dan came up beside her and wrapped an arm casually around her neck, pressing a kiss to her temple.

"Sweet tooth?"

"More like a disease. I'm a chocoholic."

"Ah, yes. I seem to remember something about that in your diary."

"Let's go before I start on a binge," Esther said, still feeling a little strange that Dan knew so much about her childhood—not exactly embarrassed anymore, but definitely strange. It seemed sort of unnatural that he should know her every childish dream, thought, and foolish act.

They were nearly out the door when Dan stopped her.

"Listen," he said, holding the door ajar, cocking his head so he could watch her face.

Esther listened. Somewhere inside the small store a radio played. She recognized the tune first and then the chorus fell into place.

Full moons and sad tunes,
And you in my arms,
Starry skies and fireflies,
And all your sweet charms.

"Boy, is that an oldie," Esther said, laughing as she walked toward the Bronco.

"Esther," Dan called after her, stretching his legs to catch up with her. "Honey, I'm sorry. I didn't mean to

America's most popular, most compelling romance novels...

Here, at last...love stories that really involve you!
Fresh, finely crafted novels with story lines so
believable you'll feel you're actually living them!
Characters you can relate to...exciting places to
visit...unexpected plot twists...all in all, exciting
romances that satisfy your mind and delight
your heart.

Get one full-length Loveswept FREE every month!
Now you can be sure you'll never, ever miss a single
Loveswept title by enrolling in our special reader's home
delivery service. A service that will bring you all six new
Loveswept romances each month for the price of five—and
deliver them to you before they appear in the bookstores!

Examine 6 Loveswept Novels for

15 days FREE!

(SEE OTHER SIDE FOR DETAILS)

upset you. I didn't even stop to think it might still hurt to hear Seth sing."

"But it doesn't," she said, giving him a small awkward smile. "I . . . it . . . that song was one of our first. It just brought back a lot of memories. I think being back here has me supersensitized to that whole time in my life."

"Can you tell me about it?" he asked gently, climbing into the Bronco beside her.

Esther laughed. "Where would I start?"

"At the beginning," Dan suggested, starting the engine up once more, eager to know the rest of Esther's story. "I know your mother once worked for Addy. Is that where she met Edgar Belldon?"

While Esther made sandwiches, peeled fruit, and popped open soft-drink cans, she told Dan that, yes, Laura had prostituted herself to Edgar Belldon. He had, according to her mother's story, claimed exclusive rights to her services at one point, leaving no doubt in Laura's mind who the father of her child was. A young, naive girl, born and raised in the hills of West Virginia, she'd gone to Edgar when she'd discovered her pregnancy. Edgar, whose wife was also pregnant with his legitimate child, had offered Laura a good job in the mine office and a house, free and clear, in return for her silence. Laura had been grateful and eternally indebted and devoted to Edgar.

"She wasn't the most liberated of women," Esther explained scornfully. "Can you imagine what a rotten year that was for ol' Edgar? Trying to keep two pregnant women on opposite ends of town happy all winter long?"

Esther's mother had cared for her, but in a sort of absent or mindless manner. She fed her, dressed her, did all the normal maintenance-type things mothers were supposed to do. But there had been no teasing, no loving, no heavy-duty discussions about life in general. There had been rules and Esther had obeyed them.

It had been Addy Markham, she went on to say, who told a terrified Esther about her life's cycles; Addy who had caught Esther pinching a chocolate bar at the variety store and made her return it and apologize. Later she treated Esther to a banana split for her courage and a promise never to steal again. It had been Addy who had held Esther while she cried the night Tommy tried to rape her, and in the end Addy Markham had been the only soul Esther had said good-bye to the night she left.

"I still can't believe that at sixteen you took the money from Gloria Belldon and left town. You must have been terrified," Dan said.

"Actually, I was mad as hell," Esther said with a shake of her head. It all seemed so long ago, and she felt so detached from it now. Still, if that was the case, why had she come back? What was she looking for now? "But if I hadn't left, Gloria was going to destroy what was left of my mother, which wasn't much after old Edgar died. You know, I really think she did love him all that time," Esther speculated.

"She loved you, too, in her way," Dan added quietly. "She told me so."

Esther's throat constricted suddenly, and she had a hard time speaking around the thickness of emotion gathering there.

"When?" she asked.

"The afternoon before the night she died. She was extremely lucid, more so than I had ever seen her. She'd had her moments of alertness before, but this was different. Even her eyes were keen and sharp instead of dreamy and dazed. She talked about her parents and your father for a while, and then said . . . and I can quote, because I've thought of it so often and wanted to tell you. She said, 'My baby Esther, such a good, sweet girl. She is the only thing in my life I'm proud of. The only worthwhile thing I've ever done was to give life to her. She never deserved all the heartache

God and me brought down on her.' " Dan glanced over at Esther and said, "Then she said that she wished she had the time to tell you she was sorry."

Esther's eyes welled with tears but they refused to fall. Her mother's words were like a salve to an open wound, but it would take time and several reapplications to heal it completely.

"She must have known she was dying," she said.

"Most people do."

They drove the length of the highway connecting Maryland and West Virginia in silence. Unlike the day before, the skies were cloudy and overcast, making the whole world seem gray and dreary. Esther hadn't even noticed the weather until now. So wrapped up in her love for Dan, she hadn't noticed the cold March wind. She'd forgotten the loneliness of her past. She had denied that both she and Dan still had major problems in their lives to solve before they could consider beginning "happily ever after."

"Tell me what happened after you left, how you met Seth," Dan asked, unable to keep from breaking the silence between them any longer.

Esther had mixed memories of her travels that got her as far as Johnson City, Tennessee, where she'd met up with a guitar-playing singer named Seth Tobin. A short time before that her suitcase and most of the money Gloria Belldon had given her had been stolen. Older than she by several years, Seth had taken pity on her. He fed her and took her to a "lady friend's" house so she could sleep safely. In return for his kindness, Esther taught him one of her songs.

"The rest is pretty much history," she said proudly.

"Come on. It can't have been all that easy in the beginning. A very young girl and an unknown singer? How did you live?" Dan asked.

Esther laughed in recollection.

"As best we could," she said. "I lied about my age for two years so I could get odd jobs. Seth got a job at a private club in Nashville. Actually that's where he met our agent, Max. He wasn't even a member of the club, just a guest and as hungry as we were. But he saw Seth's talent when no one else apparently could."

"After that we waited tables by day and played whatever gigs Max could scrape up by night. When Seth wasn't playing somewhere, I taught him my songs. Later on he made me take music classes so I could write my songs out for him to read. I graduated from the school of trial and error, but eventually I was able to do all the arrangements and orchestrations.

"Actually, those early years were harder on Seth than on me. I was so young. I did what needed to be done and sort of floated around dreaming and listening to all the music in my head. Seth was the adult, the responsible one. While I was still growing up, he was my brother, my father, my friend all wrapped up in one. He fed me, took care of me, and even though I had to work, he insisted I work only part-time. And he made me finish high school. By the time I woke up and took a real look at the world, we were halfway up the country-rock charts and cutting our first album."

"When did you marry Seth?" Dan asked, feeling invasive but knowing this was the time to ask and put his questions to rest.

"That same year. I was twenty. Seth was twenty-eight. Everything happened so fast. The album, the tour, more music, another album, we got married, went on tour again. Marrying Seth just seemed the thing to do," Esther said with a shrug.

Dan sent a frowning glance in her direction but she didn't see it. Her marriage to Seth didn't sound at all like the romantic connection Dan had read about. But before he could ask about it, Esther went on with her story.

"Those were probably my most productive years. I had old songs stored up in my head, plus new ones that seemed to come to me easily. I have to admit, though, some of those older songs were really childish and had a lot to do with my feelings about Bellewood."

"Have you written anything lately?" Dan asked with interest.

Esther stared at him for several seconds, then as if it had just occurred to her and was totally unimportant, she replied, "No. No, I haven't."

Seven

It soon became apparent to Esther that Dan's interest in her music was more than a passing curiosity.

"Damn. It's cold in here," Dan said as they entered the house through the back door. "I'll bring the rest of our stuff in if you'll turn up the heat."

He didn't linger for an answer but went back outside to empty the Bronco. Esther could have sworn they'd gotten everything on the first trip, but it wasn't really important enough to ponder. The heat, however, was.

Automatically, she made her way to the living room, where the thermostat was located.

The heat was forgotten as Esther came upon an upright piano. It had been placed in the far corner of the room near the large bay window Dan had installed to face away from the mines and out toward a view of the Alleghenies.

Slipping his arms around her waist from behind, Dan pulled her close against his chest and said, "Ta-da. I rented it in Westfield and had them deliver it yesterday. How do you like it?"

Esther was at a loss for words. Dan's gesture was incredibly generous and thoughtful and endearing, but it exerted a ton of pressure as well. It was obvious he expected her to plop herself down in front of the piano and turn out reams of music. But it was sheer torture for her to look at the instrument.

"I hope it's okay. You're probably used to better pianos, but I didn't think a baby grand would fit in here," Dan explained, sounding anxious at her continued silence.

Frantically Esther tried to find words to tell him how she felt.

Dan left her briefly, and returning from the kitchen, said, "I picked these up yesterday."

Esther turned to him. Her eyes fell to the large, familiar-looking box Dan held in his hands that she knew to be full of score sheets.

Dan took in the expression on her face. "This wasn't such a hot idea, huh?" he asked, more concerned than hurt.

"No. No," Esther quickly corrected him. "This was a terrific idea. A really wonderful and generous idea. I . . . it's . . . I'm speechless. I don't know what to say."

Dan took heart. "Don't say anything. Give me a kiss and then go work your fingers to the bone."

Esther complied readily with the kiss, a sincere thank-you for his loving heart, but she procrastinated about approaching the piano.

"I don't think I'll be able to work with you in the house. We talented artists are very temperamental. And you are . . . distracting," she said as she outlined the shape of his sensuous lips with her index finger.

Dan appeared to like her description of him, because he grinned.

"In what way?" he asked as he ran his hands over her hips and up her sides to a sensitive area near her breasts.

"Um . . ." Esther had to think fast. "All your reading. The sound of pages turning would drive me nuts."

Dan pulled her closer while he slipped one hand

around her breast and began a slow descent across her stomach and upper thigh.

"Anything else?" he asked wickedly.

"Ah . . . well, if you move around in the house, I'll hear you and lose my concentration."

Dan lowered his head to make little swirls with his tongue along Esther's neck.

"I'll take up yoga," he offered. "Meditate while you work."

"The humming . . . would . . . disturb me," Esther murmured.

"I'll hum in my head," Dan promised as he nibbled at her lower lip.

Esther was already humming in her head, and as far as she was concerned, the debate was over. He certainly was a distraction.

Dan, however, felt he was the true winner. Esther was proving to be the most sensual woman he'd ever known. Each new lovemaking session was an adventure into exquisite delight. She used her body to drive him to near madness, while her own unguarded responses encouraged his imagination to seek out new heights of rapture for them to share.

That night they ate dinner in Bellewood at a small café that had changed very little since Addy had taken Esther there to celebrate her sixteenth birthday. Addy had given her the hairbrush as a birthday gift, and only a few months later Esther had left Bellewood behind her.

Things were different now. People stopped to say hello. They were friendly and cordial in a natural way, making very little fuss over Esther's success or her history. Treating both Dan and Esther with neighborly respect and thoughtfulness, they were neither gushy nor condescending, simply curious. So what was she waiting for, Esther wondered.

Deep within her was a fourteen-year-old girl with her fists up, prepared to battle against the slights and slurs she knew were coming, had learned to expect and defend herself and her mother against.

When Dan offered her a penny for her thoughts, Esther laughed at her foolishness and shook her head.

"Some things never change, Esther. Some things do," he said once he'd gotten his penny's worth. "There are still women who use their bodies to get what they want or need. There are still men with no integrity. But you've changed, and although it's probably taken Bellewood longer to catch up with the times, it's changed too. If you'd been born ten or fifteen years later, your life would have been totally different, I'm sure."

Esther was thoughtful. What would her life have been like if her childhood had been as easy as Jewel Belldon's? What kind of music would she have written if she hadn't had to use it as an outlet for her emotions? Would she have married a hard-working miner and been the happy mother of eight when Dan came to town as the temporary doctor?

Up to his old trick of reading her mind, Dan went on to say, "There's a rhyme and reason for most everything in life. We just never figure it out until after we've already dealt with it the hard way."

Later Dan dropped her off at the house and left to check on his housebound patients. Esther was alone in her mother's old house once again. Alone with her thoughts and the disquieting silence of the piano in the corner. Without Dan's presence to keep her mind occupied, the doubts and fears crept forward to prey on her consciousness.

Hoping for an answer, even a small clue, she read her diary aloud from beginning to end and found the girl she had once been.

"The Reverend Mr. Jamison says God made all things.

So He must have made me too. And He wouldn't have put such beautiful music in me if I weren't a good person. I don't think I'm the curse of my mama's wickedness. I think I'm someone special.

"I'm going to leave Bellewood someday. And I won't ever come back here. I'm going to be rich too. I'll send for Mama and she can come live with me in my beautiful house. Maybe when she sees how famous and rich I am, she'll be proud of me. . . . I had a fight with Jewel Avery today. I made her nose bleed. She said I'd grow up to be a whore like my mama. I told her that was a lie and to take it back but she wouldn't. She just said it again, over and over. Mama locked my bedroom door. I'm very hungry but I don't think Jewel will call me names anymore . . ."

> I'll have the world at my feet
> I'll be someone to meet,
> I'll have someone to love,
> I'll thank the heavens above,
> I'll have it all. I'll have it all.
>
> I'll have a house on the beach,
> I'll be so hard to reach,
> I'll never be blue or lonely,
> I'll be his one and only,
> I'll have it all. I'll have it all.
>
> I'll be laughing someday,
> I'll hear these folks stop and say,
> We didn't know what we had,
> This kid, she isn't so bad,
> I'll have it all. I'll have it all. . . .

"Old Man Belldon came to call again. He wanted to know if there was anything he could do to make up for what he and Tommy did to me. I didn't like asking, but I told him about the special music school in Charleston that Addy told me about. He said people would talk if I went off to a school like that. I told him I didn't care what people said about me. So he explained how important he was and how everyone's job would be in danger if people started saying bad things about him and how much it would hurt him and Mama and his family. In the end, I told him that if he couldn't send me to school, there was nothing he could do to make up for being my father or for what Tommy did and that he didn't look very important from where I stood. . . .

"There are so many things I want to do. The world is so much bigger than Bellewood. I want to see all of it. I want to do everything. I want to fall in love someday like the ladies in Addy's novels do. I want a baby of my own, lots of them like Mrs. Fischer has. I'll hug them and kiss them, and they'll know I love them. I'll make my dreams come true. I know in my heart I can do it. . . .

"My father had a heart attack today. He died. It's too bad I can't say I'll miss him. Mama's real upset. Said it was all my fault for not forgiving him when he asked me to. She says he died of a broken heart because of me. I think he just drank too much. . . ."

Esther almost envied the girl in the diary. There was some quality in her that as a woman she'd misplaced. What was it? The hope for greater days? The determination and strength? The will to succeed? It was hard to tell. She liked to think all those qualities still existed in her, but she hadn't tested herself lately to find out. All she knew for sure was that she'd lost the edge she'd had before. She was reluctant, almost fearful of going back to the life she'd led before the accident. The music that had always been there bubbling up from her heart, playing in the back of her mind, wasn't there, she realized with a lonely, abandoned feeling.

It was getting late. Dan would be home soon. Esther longed for the comfort and security of his loving arms. She needed to feel the steady thumping of his heart next to hers, hear its reassuring rhythm.

Although she knew she ought to go to bed, her body tense, aching, and exhausted from the trip, her mind was wide awake and active. The memories, the emotions, the questions, and what few answers she'd found goaded her to push forward with still more questions. But they were melting together and falling apart, becoming more and more confusing.

Aimlessly she wandered the house until she found herself in Dan's study. She recalled the nights and lazy afternoons Dan had held her in his arms while they watched movies or comedy specials on his video recorder. Perhaps she'd find something tranquilizing enough in his varied collection to stop her circling thoughts, something she could watch mindlessly until her brain realized it was as tired as her body.

She browsed through the collection of movies and taped documentaries, noting the possibilities as she went, until she came to a cassette with an unmarked cover. She removed the tape and found it labeled: ESTHER.

Naturally she popped the tape into the machine and turned the system on. It was a late night talk show on which Seth had been a guest, singing their latest hit. The host made a brief reference to the fact that she was waiting in the Green Room, after which Seth made a husbandly comment about watching his words or walking home after the show. Esther remembered the program well, even though it happened four or five years before and had been one of many such shows. She smiled at the jokes and double-talk between Seth and the host, who had come to be their friend over the years.

The tape fuzzed, then moved into a music video production they had done nearly four years earlier.

> Love . . . don't be leaving me.
> Stay . . . believe in me tonight.

Seth sang the words to a tender melody as he walked

through a city in the early morning hours, alone on the deserted streets. It had been Chicago, Esther recalled, and the police had barricaded various streets at different locations for nearly a week during the middle of the night so they could tape the video.

> Love, I won't be leaving you,
> I believe in you,
> So hold on tight, tonight.

It was a good video, but Esther couldn't help remembering that Seth had felt so foolish wandering around mouthing the words to a tape player.

Then came a twenty-minute in-depth, personal interview with the two of them by a female reporter. It had been part of a TV special. There were shots of a pregnant Esther in a sound booth working on the final orchestration that would back up Seth's voice in their latest hit single.

Engrossed, Esther was only partially aware that Dan was home and was watching her watch herself on television. Quietly he crossed the room and without a word sat down beside her, stretching a protective arm across the back of the couch.

Together they viewed parts of the recording session showing Esther cuing Seth, rocking to the rhythm of the song and smiling her encouragement from the sound booth. There was a clip from the Grammy Awards three years previously in which they'd taken home the Best Male Vocalist award for the second time and the Song of the Year award for the third time. Esther remembered it well. Then the interview began. The camera had taken shots of Seth, Esther, and Donny—then just six months old. They talked about the thrill of parenthood, the changes in their lives, the good fortune they'd had, and their hopes for the future.

Dan felt Esther flinch as Seth Tobin began singing their now famous, final musical effort.

Together we'll take what life brings,
Gentle breezes and glorious springs.
Together we'll weather the storms,
Because our love protects us; a barrier forms.

There on the screen were candid shots of Esther and her son playing on the beach, running in the waves, laughing and happy. Seth joined them, and the three of them frolicked, while verse after verse of the joyous song was sung.

You, me, and our love,
Are blessed from above,
We'll cherish it, nurture it, a wonderful thing,
A lifetime together to make our hearts sing.

By the time it was over, there were tears on Esther's cheeks. She sat silently crying, watching as the video faded and went blank. Dan reached for the remote control and turned the system off.

"I'm sorry," Dan said, pulling her close and letting her cry. "You must miss Seth a lot."

First Esther shook her head, then she nodded.

"I do miss him," she said in a weepy voice. "He was the best friend I ever had. He . . . he was a terrific person, and I do miss him a lot."

Dan handed her his handkerchief. She wiped her eyes to temporarily stop the flow and gently blew her nose.

"But Seth had done it all." She went on talking about her grief for the first time since the accident. "He used to say that if he died tomorrow, he'd die a happy man. He'd accomplished his life's goal, loved a good woman, and fathered a son. He used to say that life didn't get any better than what we already had." She took a jagged breath and went on. "To console myself, I like to think he died while he was at the top, loved and admired. He didn't have to grow old and watch his career decline over the years. I took a certain comfort in knowing he was happy when he died. Somehow it made accepting his death a little easier."

Dan was taking comfort as well, listening to her words. One of his greatest fears had been the possibility that she wasn't over her husband's death, that her wounds were still too tender to allow her to give herself to another man.

It was selfish of him, he knew, but it made him happy to hear her speak of her relationship with her husband, to know hers had been a good marriage based on mutual trust and respect and need, a friendship with strongly binding ties they'd both been content with. It hadn't held a tempestuous passion or a bonding of souls that deep true love brought. It simply had been a fond partnership that had suited their needs both professionally and personally.

"But Donny," Esther uttered, beginning to cry anew, her tears bitter. "Oh, my baby Donny. He was so beautiful and so happy. I ache so much to have my baby back."

Racked with pain, Esther leaned into Dan, seeking his strength, sharing her pain, allowing him to console her. When at last her sobs weakened and her tears dried, she began to speak in a dull, numb voice.

"We were going to our producer's house for dinner. He lived up in the hills. I took my own car because I needed to run an errand, and if Donny got tired, I could bring him home early for bed. Something went wrong. Seth lost control of the car and went over the embankment. The whole thing was so useless and stupid. My baby never had a chance," she said limply, her eyes dazed.

Dan felt her agony and her loss, and even though he'd tried to comfort others in their grief, he could find no words for Esther. He could only agree with her, feel for her, and stay with her until she was able to cope.

He kissed her temple lovingly and held her close. She

was cool and moist and beginning to shiver over the outpouring of her memories. Briefly he left her to get some brandy. He pressed the glass to her lips and forced her to take several large gulps. Esther coughed and grimaced as the smooth liquor assaulted her system, and she looked vaguely at Dan as if seeing him for the first time since he'd entered the room nearly an hour earlier.

Dan bent and scooped Esther into his arms. She laid her head on his shoulder, helpless and despondent, and sighed. "I'm sorry. It still hurts."

"I know, sweetheart. It's okay," he murmured softly against her cheek. He hit the light switch on the wall with his shoulder to darken the room, then made his way to Esther's. "I just wish I could help."

"You have," she replied, her voice still distant.

Dan laid Esther on the bed and pulled the covers out from under her. With the clinical hands of a doctor he gently removed her socks and jeans. He helped her up so he could remove her sweater and bra. Carefully he covered her. Then he undressed himself and slid in beside her. With the arms of a tender, caring man, he embraced her, holding her close, warming her body with his. He stroked her body from shoulder to hip, soothing and reassuring her. And with a lover's heart he cherished her while she slept.

Just as the sun began to rise above the mountains and daylight began to fade the darkness of night, when shadows weren't quite visible and solid forms were only slightly darker than the lightness they stood in, Esther dozed in that state of mind where she wasn't really asleep but wasn't quite awake either.

She was aware of the warmth and lassitude that permeated her body, the feeling of belonging that filled her heart and eased her mind. She moved closer to the source of her contentment and felt arms tighten around her, holding her close, protecting her.

The image of a dark-haired man with fathomless eyes and an engaging smile surfaced in her mind's eye. She reached for his broad, muscled shoulders and ran her hand over his back. He was firm and strong and so real to her in her dreaminess.

Lips were pressed to the base of her neck. They instigated a series of little shivers that ran over her shoulder and down to her breasts. They moved up and around to below her ear, causing Esther to shudder with the repeated sensations.

"Are you all right, Esther?" Dan whispered close to her ear.

The voice disturbed her dream and she came fully awake. Recalling the night before but not moving, she refused to give up all the good feelings of the moment.

"Where did you get that tape?" she asked quietly, not angry or suspicious, simply wanting to know.

"I made it. I have all your albums too," he volunteered.

"Why?"

Dan took a deep breath to bolster his courage.

"You're going to think I'm insane," he said. "I've been hopelessly in love with you for years. No," he said, holding her closer, "don't pull away from me. It's not what you're thinking."

"I'm just surprised," Esther said, moving back into his embrace willingly. She trusted him completely. He'd already proven his worthiness to her by saving her life and keeping the secrets of her diary. And she knew she could trust his feelings for her. They weren't related to her fame or fortune; instinctively, she knew they were for her. "I didn't think you even liked me very much when we first met."

"Self-defense," he explained. "I didn't want to throw myself at your feet like a crazed fan. I wanted you to have time to get to know me. To know me as well as I knew you." He paused to press a gentle kiss to her temple, then went on. "And I do know you, Esther. Better than I've ever known another human being. I don't care what you do, but I love who you are. Your face is beautiful and I want your body so badly, I can hardly think of anything else. But it's what's inside you I love. I admire and respect your intelligence and determination. I adore your wit and gentleness, and I'm in awe of your capacity to forgive and to be optimistic. I feel like I've known you forever, and I want you in my future. I need you in my life, Esther."

"And I want you in mine," Esther said, insinuating a leg between his and pressing closer. "I have so much love to give you."

Dan hugged her to him tightly until she was nearly breathless, then relaxed a bit.

"I know you do," he said, deeply moved. "We're going to have such a wonderful life. We'll have babies and raise then together, grow gray-haired together and—"

"Dan," Esther interrupted in a knee-jerk reaction to his plans. "I . . . I'm not sure I want another baby."

Dan's hands were comforting as they moved up and down her back while he smiled in the grayness of the early morning. He knew his Esther and he knew there would be children.

"That's up to you, sweetheart. You're all I want or need to make me happy. Just say we can plan to grow old together, that we can buy rocking chairs and listen to each other's arteries harden for the next few hundred years."

"Will I have to get dentures?"

"Not if you don't want to. We could live on a banana farm," he said teasing. Sheathing his teeth with his lips and bringing himself up to lean over Esther, he said, "I won't get any either and we'll give each other mushy kisses like this . . ."

Esther giggled at his antics. But when he persisted in his sloppy kissing routine, she dug her fingers into his sides, causing him to convulse violently and pull away.

"What's this?" Esther asked in mock surprise. "Does the master have a weakness?"

"No," Dan lied, straightfaced.

"Are you sure?"

"Very."

"Let's see," she said boldly.

Esther reached out to poke him in the side, but he moved back quickly. Taking an attack position on her hands and knees, she stalked him over the short distance between them in the bed very carefully.

"Esther," he said, using her name as a warning. "Revenge is sweet."

Esther moved closer.

"Esther."

She made her best move, but Dan proved to be a worthy opponent. With very little effort he had her by the wrists and was pulling her upward against his chest. With his legs between hers, he suddenly sat up. Curling his long legs Indian-style under Esther's bottom, he kept her in his lap. Releasing her wrists for the briefest of seconds, he wound her legs around him then returned to secure her wrists.

"Now I'll show you just how sweet revenge can be," Dan said wickedly.

Although the position seemed awkward at first, Esther soon found there was a method to Dan's madness. Holding her arms loosely but securely at the small of her back, Dan had total and perfect access to Esther's breasts. Placing his open mouth over one rosy tip, he began to suck and brush his tongue against her nipple until Esther shuddered. She groaned her pleasure and arched her back in encouragement.

Dan moved down her exposed abdomen to lave her navel with his tongue before moving to the opposite breast. There he performed much the same careful ministrations designed to drive Esther mad with passion and need.

Esther felt like a loose live wire full of high-voltage energy with no way of releasing it, nowhere to channel it. In her need she began to fidget and writhe wantonly against Dan's hard, strong body, silently begging for deliverance.

Releasing one of Esther's hands, which she instantly moved to the back of his head to draw him even closer to her breasts, Dan slid his hand between her legs to find yet another source of electrical generation, filling Esther to the point of overload.

With insanity closing in, Esther cried out in agony and Dan was there to ease her pain. He guided her hips to his ready point of relief and thrust deeply within her. Together they discharged the energy built up within them, until at last the currents between them were again calm and running smoothly.

"In all my wildest dreams and fantasies of loving you like this, it was never this wonderful," Dan murmured a short while later as he leaned back against the pillows, Esther's body sprawled across his.

"I never even dreamed *anything* could be this wonderful," she mumbled lazily against his chest.

"I love you so much, Esther," Dan said, a quiver of emotion slipping thickly into his voice.

Esther looked up to him then, and with the early morning sunlight filtering into the room, she could see the depth and seriousness of his words in his expression.

"And I love you, Dan Jacobey—so much it scares me."

Eight

March became early April. Winter snow melted into spring and with it came the rains. For days on end the rain came in sheets, beating open the dogwood blossoms, pulling color from the land, dispelling the winter's dreariness.

Esther had always loved these spring showers. There was something cleansing and renewing about them, and even though they diluted the ground into a marshy bog, her heart was light as she watched the heralding of spring.

"It rains like this in California too. Harder even, sometimes," she told Eddy Belldon as she held the door wide for one of his frequent visits.

Dan was in Westfield for the morning picking up a shipment of medical supplies he'd ordered. Esther was alone with the piano and couldn't have been more happy or relieved to hear Eddy's motorcycle turn off the access road.

"How come you aren't in school today?"

"The low bridge into Buckton is covered, so us Bellwood kids got the day off. We'll have to make up the work later," Eddy informed her as he entered through the kitchen door at the rear of the house where he'd parked his motorcycle.

As Esther recalled, "low bridge" days were fairly common. A six- or seven-foot rise in the river was expected with heavy rainfall. The larger city of Westfield, on the Bellewood side of the bridge, was where most of the townspeople did their out-of-the-ordinary shopping. So the flooding of the low bridge was of little consequence to the miners. The children certainly didn't mind an extra day or two away from school. And Esther could feel sure of seeing Dan at lunchtime, because he didn't have to go anywhere near the river or the flooded bridge.

Eddy came to call quite often after school or on weekend afternoons. It had taken several visits before he'd felt comfortable enough with Esther to come inside. Esther was glad the days of suffering the elements to talk to him were over with no sign of the relapse Dan had predicted. Glad, too, that Eddy felt he could trust her.

Whether his initial uneasiness was due to her fame or to things his parents had told him about her, Esther would never know. But it no longer mattered because his uneasiness no longer existed. Eddy now spoke freely with her, expressing his ambitions and hopes, even going so far as to tease and joke with her. Esther found herself growing very attached to the intelligent, sensitive young man Eddy was proving himself to be. In an odd sort of way, she found he had a lot in common with the sixteen-year-old girl in her diary.

On this visit he'd brought with him a package wrapped in brown paper, which he was careful not to bump or bang on his way in.

"And don't lecture me about riding my bike in the rain, 'cuz I was real careful," he went on to say, apparently accepting the fact that she was an adult and therefore subject to strange mental processes.

"You're also soaking wet," she said.

"I'll dry."

"You will dry. In the bathroom. And put on Dan's bathrobe while I throw your clothes in the dryer," Esther said, not uncomfortable with pulling rank on him or with the fact that she cared about her nephew's health.

His protests were shortlived. Esther made tea with lots of cream and sugar—the way he liked it—while he changed. He emerged from the bathroom wearing Dan's robe and his own boots, feeling and looking quite silly.

Esther took his jeans, jacket, and shirt.

"Where are your socks?" she questioned.

"In my boots."

"Are they wet?"

"A little."

"Hand 'em over."

With his clothes in the dryer and a pair of Dan's socks on his feet, they moved to the warmth of the living room, where, once again, Eddy was very careful of the package he'd brought with him.

When Esther expressed curiosity, he said, "I found it in our attic a long time ago and I wanted you to see it. But first I want to ask you something."

"Shoot," Esther replied as she curled her legs beneath her on the couch and gave him her undivided attention.

"Who are you?" he asked bluntly. "I mean, who are you really? How come my folks hate you so much?"

Taken aback not for the first time by his tactlessness but most certainly by his question, Esther was silent for several seconds. A heavy mental debate ensued and finally she decided to be as honest with him as possible without going into detail.

"You must know that my mother wasn't married when she had me, and before that she was a prositute . . . like Addy Markham used to be," she explained unemotionally. "Things today are a little different, but when I was growing up here, unwed mothers and their children were considered to be real lowlifes. But my mother had a pretty good job at the mines, and I had a tendency to think I was as good as anyone else and people resented it. Your parents included. They weren't any different from the rest of the people in Bellewood, Eddy. That's just the way things were then."

"So why do they still hate you?"

"I don't know. I didn't know why they hated me then. Maybe they still dislike me because of the way they were taught to feel. If their opinions have changed, maybe they're just embarrassed by the way they were before," she said, trying with all her might to be charitable, adding a shrug to convey the unimportance of it all.

"There's more to it than that," Eddy said knowingly.

Esther frowned. It was hard to defend Tom and Jewel Belldon. Their antagonism was long-lived and deep-rooted. But something inside her couldn't bring forth enough hatred to destroy Eddy's opinion of his parents.

"Well, kids do mean things to other children. Especially when they're young and don't know any better," she explained simply.

"Hey, you two, what's up?" Dan asked as he entered the room, home for the lunch that had totally slipped Esther's mind. Looking from face to face, he, too, frowned and asked, "What's so serious? Have I interrupted something deep?"

"Yes."

"No." They answered according to their own view.

To Dan's questioning expression Esther explained, "We were talking about the relationship between me and his parents."

"And she wasn't telling me the whole truth," Eddy said accusingly.

Dan and Esther exchanged glances, instantly knowing the other's thoughts. With his suspicions apparently confirmed, Eddy turned to the package beside him and tore off the brown paper.

"Who are you really, Esther?" he asked again more pointedly.

Eddy had unwrapped a small portrait of Esther . . . or someone who looked very much like her in appearance. Wide-eyed and open-mouthed, Esther rose from the couch and knelt beside Eddy to take a closer look.

The woman possessed the straight, thick black hair of the Belldons and of Esther Brite, but unlike the cool blue eyes of Tom Belldon and old Edgar before him, this woman had long, almond-shaped green-gold eyes— eyes as exotic and keen and bright as Esther's own.

"Good Lord," Dan said. "Who is she? Where did you get this?"

"She's my dad's great-grandmother. She was Ukrainian. I looked her up in my grandfather's Bible, where he had this family tree thing. I think her name was Mesha."

Esther sat back on her legs and looked from the picture to Eddy.

"Could you rephrase your question, please?" she asked, a smile signaling her defeat.

"How are we related?" Eddy asked.

"Your grandfather was my father. I'm your father's half sister. I'm your aunt," she stated. "Okay?"

"Okay!" He grinned and nodded his approval. His features changed suddenly with an afterthought. "Does Dad know?"

"If he's never seen this, he may not. Your grandma went to a lot of trouble to protect him from the truth," she said.

"Is she why you left?"

Covering only the high points, Esther briefly told her story. When she was finished, there was a sort of warm admiration in Eddy's eyes and a happy acknowledgment of the bond between them. He dressed and prepared to go, intending to leave the portrait behind. When Esther protested, he still refused to take it back.

"That thing was covered with cobwebs when I found it as a little kid. The first time I saw a picture of you in a magazine, I went up to the attic and hid it. It was my big secret for a long, long time, You keep it. I don't think my folks even know it exists," he said, then waved and called, "See ya later, Auntie Esther."

"That's for private use only," Esther cautioned. Eddy grinned his pledge.

"You're a classy lady, Auntie Esther," Dan commented over lunch a short while later.

It would have been so easy for her to tear Tom Belldon to shreds in front of his son. That she hadn't even considered it spoke volumes on her character.

"Yes, I know," Esther said with exaggerated self-indulgence. "And I do believe my karma is charged for life. I may never have to do another good deed to get into heaven."

"Good. Then I'll go with you," Dan said excitedly.

"Where?"

"Up to the Big House so you can throw that picture in Tom Belldon's face."

The fact that Dan would enjoy putting the Belldons in their place amused Esther, that he wanted to do it for her sake was endearing. However, her expression was gently disapproving when she spoke.

"What would it prove? That our father was a spineless, unfaithful womanizer? That my blood is just as good as Tom's? I've known that for years, long before I met my father."

"Yeah, but wouldn't it be great to watch Tom squirm the way he's made you squirm."

Esther got up to remove their plates and get coffee.

"You'd love rubbing his nose in it, wouldn't you," she commented, only half teasing.

"Yeah, I'm afraid I would," he admitted. "However, since it is your choice," he said, watching her set the coffee on the table, then taking her by the arm and pulling her into his lap, "I'll settle for rubbing my own nose in something far more enjoyable."

He did so between Esther's breast. Even through the tailored blouse and the lightweight sweater she wore, Esther could feel the heat of his breath against her skin. His playfulness inflamed the rosy glow of happiness that had been her constant companion over the past several weeks.

Esther laughed and palmed his face, effectively diverting his attention.

"Lord, man, don't you think of anything but sex?" she asked.

"Not if I know I'm within ten miles of you."

He started rubbing her neck with his nose and added a little intimate nibbling while he was there. "Besides, I'll bet you can't think of any two things better to think about," he challenged.

"Sure I can."

"Let's hear 'em."

"Well, there's the appointment as chief surgeon at the trauma center in D.C.," she said lightly, not sure how he'd respond to the subject.

"That's not better than sex," he said, his eyes opening to take in the concern and seriousness on her face.

"It is something else to think about though."

"And I am thinking about it, sweetheart. I'm still leery. I'm so afraid of letting the pain take over again. I hated the unfeeling man it drove me to become."

"If you're aware of the danger and afraid of it, you won't let it happen," Esther said, trying to console him.

"And what about you? Would you come with me and write your music in Washington?"

"If you wanted me to."

"Did you get much done today, or did Eddy take up most of your morning?" Dan asked, his confidence in her and her talent unwavering.

Esther hated letting him think she spent every moment he was away cultivating her creative genius. But she couldn't admit to herself that her music was gone . . . how could she admit it to him? How could she explain that the emotions were there, stronger and more alive than ever before because of him, but the vehicle she used best to express them was out of commission, that she was so afraid of failing on her own, that somewhere along the line she had turned her music off. She ached to turn it back on now but was too afraid it wouldn't be the same.

"I . . . I'm having sort of a hard time settling down and getting serious about it," she said, glazing over the truth. "I think I have spring fever."

"Ah, yes. Spring. That time of year when everything is birds and bees. And love and making love are in the air." He waxed poetic to get them back on his original track of thinking.

Dan took the lobe of Esther's ear between his teeth and tugged gently, urging her to follow along in his scheme. Esther laughed her unfought defeat and began to drop soft little kisses over his face.

Dan, craving more sustenance, finally found her mouth, savoring the sweet taste of her, growing heady on the smell that was uniquely hers. His fingertips tingled with anticipation as they moved under her sweater and beneath her blouse to touch the warm silkiness of her skin.

They both heard the rumble as it moved off the access road onto the dirt drive toward the house. Resigned to a temporary delay in their pleasure, they looked at each other promisingly, while Eddy's motorcycle ground down to a halt at the back door.

"Doc! Doc!" The boy burst in without knocking, too

agitated to realize what he'd interrupted. "You'd better come quick. The river's flooded higher than I've ever seen it. Most of the river houses are falling apart. Some are down already. People are standing in the streets crying, Esther. The whole place is full of mud and there's garbage everywhere."

By Eddy's reaction, Esther rather calmly calculated that the river hadn't flooded in the last five years. During the last flood Esther's mother had seemed to rally in the crisis, opening her house to the homeless, feeding them, caring for the young while the adults had gone out to salvage what was left of their lives. That flooding season had been the first and last time Esther had ever felt real pride in her mama.

Dan was on his feet before the significance of Eddy's words had truly registered in Esther's mind. In what seemed like a dream, he went to both bedrooms and the hall closet, gathering extra blankets and large towels, his flashlight, medical bag, and extra supplies. He was pulling on his coat when it finally clicked in Esther's head that she could be of help at the flood site as well, that all of this was real. The river had flooded again.

Throwing on her coat and reaching for her boots, Esther came up short when Dan took her by the shoulders and looked her square in the face.

"You're staying here," he said firmly, his face deadly serious.

"Don't be silly. I want to help."

"No. Stay here, where you'll be safe. I don't want to have to worry about you. Please. Stay here."

"But that's—"

"Esther, there's no time to argue. Please stay here and be safe."

And with that he was out the door. Esther only stood and sputtered for a second or two, then marched out into the rain just as Dan was pulling away.

"Stay here," he shouted from the window of the

Bronco, then he turned to speak to Eddy, who had obviously decided to go back to town with Dan rather than risk another motorcycle trip.

Esther was very angry. Loving her was one thing, but bossing her around, treating her like a complete incompetent, and walking out in the middle of an argument were altogether a different matter.

Back inside, she found boxes and loaded them with coffee and milk and juice mixes, everything she thought might be needed or useful. Laboriously she carried each heavy box out to her little red sports car, which was sheltered in a carport on the far side of the house.

Esther hadn't been anywhere alone in her car since the day Dan brought her home unconscious and near death with pneumonia two months earlier. She made several efforts to start the engine before it came to life and purred powerfully.

It seemed, however, that the whole world was conspiring against her, when no more than twenty feet away from the carport she became deeply and hopelessly stuck in the mud.

Expletives fell from her mouth as she struggled to get out of the car, slamming the door closed with her foot before slogging back through the rain and the mud into the house.

Fit to be tied, she went to the phone for help only to discover that the line was dead.

"Damn you, Dan," she shouted in the general direction of town, loud enough for him to hear her, she thought. "Why the hell didn't you take me with you?"

At first she was sure she imagined it. Then she heard the sound again and again. Someone was honking a horn out on the access road.

"Your little red bullet ain't much use up here, is it, Esther Brite?" Addy Markham called out, laughing merrily while Esther loaded the last of the three boxes into Addy's big Buick and crawled limply in beside her.

"We were sabotaged," Esther said, breathing heavily. "And I did notice you didn't drive this Sherman tank off the paved road."

"And get stuck in the mud? Not me, little girl," Addy said, laughing heartily at Esther's foolishness and frustration.

The older woman put her car in gear and made her way down the mountain into Bellewood. They saw the river first. Through the trees they could see beyond the town, where it flowed around a bend in the valley surrounding Bellewood.

Normally a slow-moving river, it now moved rapidly, throwing whitecaps to show its anger and strength. It carried felled trees and tons of dirt like twigs and sand.

When Bellewood came into view, Addy stopped briefly to survey the damage. Most of the town was essentially intact, but the row of houses that had been built close to the river was only partially standing, some structures just a pile of debris, others no longer there at all.

The river had risen thirty to forty feet past the original riverbank. Esther could see movement on what had been River Street, a gravel road between the two rows of houses running parallel to the river. There were a couple of small boats out on the swollen river. Esther worried that Dan might be in one, but she was too far away to tell.

Already volunteers had established themselves in the town hall. Flood victims stood in small groups or alone with devastated expressions on their faces. Women were crying and several of the miners stomped around angrily. Older children, aware of what had happened, sat bewildered and idle, while the younger ones appeared to be having quite a good time chasing one another about the hall. Babies cried or slept passively in their mothers' arms. All were dirty and mud-caked. They all looked tired and cold.

Delivering the food she had brought to the small kitchen off the meeting hall, Esther soon found her hands filled with thick paper cups and a thermos of hot coffee. She passed among the gathering offering hot drinks and solving what immediate problems she could—a blanket for warmth; finger food for a toothless toddler; a corner to lie down in and rest; analgesics for tension headaches.

Time passed swiftly for Esther, but she was sure it just crawled by for the women who waited anxiously for word of their husbands and homes. The first chance she got to look up and note the hour, she was stunned. Nearly eight hours had passed and night had fallen.

Neighbors began to take in neighbors, splitting up families when it was necessary. Spare sleeping bags and blankets were brought in for those who were left, who would take shelter in the hall and be grateful that they and their loved ones were still alive.

Esther worked tirelessly, and the people accepted her as part of the community. They didn't comment on her fame or her past. She was simply Esther, as if she'd always been among them.

Esther was putting several children to bed, when her skin began to prickle. She looked up to see Dan standing in the foyer talking to several of the men. Eddy was with him and spotted her first. He made a short wave of recognition before giving Dan a nudge.

Following the boy's directions, Dan's gaze locked with Esther's. No recriminations or guilt passed between them, only the heartfelt joy of seeing each other again, safe and unharmed.

As if by mutual consent, they made their way to one of the few relatively isolated spaces left in the hall. Standing near the lavatories, with people coming and going, they embraced.

"Don't you ever do that again. I was so mad I could have spit," Esther said.

Knowing exactly what she meant, Dan squeezed her a little tighter and said, "I just wanted you out of harm's way. I love you."

"Well, I wasn't planning to go out with the rescue team. I just wanted to help."

"Tom Belldon's out and about too," Dan added. His opinion that Tom Belldon was as lethal as the flood was clear in his voice.

"That *is* terrifying," Esther said theatrically. "But I can handle him too."

Dan's eyes twinkled with pride and humor.

"Pretty tough little cookie, aren't you?"

"Yeah."

"So what happened to your car?"

"Oh. You've been up to the house."

Dan nodded. "I found a job for you. When I saw the beached red whale, I guessed what you were up to and came looking for you."

"Addy brought me down."

"Good. She looks tired. So do you. I want you to take Addy and the baby home. Try to get some rest, too, though."

"What baby?" Esther asked, frowning. She had been so glad to see him, it wasn't until that moment that Esther noticed how tense and agitated Dan was. His words, although showing his concern and some humor, were clipped and had seemed forced. It became more and more apparent that he was under a great deal of stress. "What's wrong, Dan? What's happened to you? Does it have anything to do with this baby you were talking about?"

"Shhh. I'm fine. Really," Dan assured her, lowering his voice. "I'm tired and—"

"No. There's more to it. Talk to me."

Dan looked around the room uncomfortably, stalling

for words. He needed Esther's faith and reassurance but didn't know how to ask for them. Finally he took her hand and said, "Come on. Let's go outside for a minute."

The rain had slackened to a drizzle. The wind, however, continued to blow cold air that seemed to move straight through Esther and cling to her bones.

The Bronco was parked in a no-parking zone directly in front of the hall. Dan reached in and pulled out a blanket. He was careful not to slam the door, then turned and wrapped Esther first in the blanket and then in his arms. For several long minutes he held her without speaking.

Esther could feel the turmoil in him and longed to ease his suffering. With all her might she tried to convey to him through their embrace that all she was, all she had was his.

"We found a man and his daughter trapped under some pilings a little while ago. He's in bad shape. The child looks okay. She's worn out, but nothing's broken. Wake her up a little every hour or so just to make sure, though. There . . . there's a mother . . . but no one has seen her." Dan increased the strength of his hold on Esther. "I'm going to operate on the father. He's at the clinic now getting a transfusion; hopefully it will stabilize him a little. He's bleeding internally . . . lost a lot . . ."

The meaning of what he was saying finally became clear to Esther. Dan hadn't performed more than the simplest of operations in five years, and he was frightened. So much so, his speech was disjointed and confusing.

"At first I thought we could get him to Westfield, but I don't think there's time. I—"

"You can do it, Dan. I haven't a doubt," Esther said simply, pulling away to show him the confidence of her conviction. "I don't know anything about surgery, but if you tell me what to do, I'll try to help you."

A wonderfully strange expression came over Dan's face. The profound tenderness and amazement in his eyes shook Esther deeply.

"You really would, wouldn't you?"

"Of course I would. I believe in you. I know you can do it. I'd be there only to hand you those little pincher things," Esther said.

Dan laughed.

"One of the miners was a paramedic in 'Nam during the war. He's offered to hand me the 'little pincher things.' Acutally, he'll probably be more at home than I will under these conditions."

Dan took Esther by the shoulders then and gripped them encouragingly.

"I do have a favor to ask of you, though," he continued uncertainly. "I want you to take the little girl home and take care of her. Get Addy to take you back and ask her to stay the night. Can you do that for me?"

"Sure," Esther said easily, surprised that he thought she might not.

With the greatest of care Dan reopened the door of the Bronco. Reaching inside, he withdrew what appeared to be a blanket. Upon closer inspection Esther realized it was actually a baby who couldn't have been more than a year old.

Esther's heart sank with despair, and panic rose up inside her. All afternoon she'd warmed bottles and food and found diapers and clothing for the babies inside the hall. And all afternoon she'd gone out of her way, consciously, to avoid having to hold any of them. Opportunities had certainly arisen, and without much effort she had ignored them. She hadn't held a baby since she'd held Donny. She had no desire to do so now. In fact, she was quite loath to the idea.

"She's a baby," Esther stated the obvious with near contempt in her tone.

"Eleven months old. She'll be starving when she wakes

up, so scrounge up a bottle before you go home," Dan told her distractedly. "Esther. I wouldn't ask this of you if I didn't have to. The other people in town have their hands full already, and I . . . I promised her father I'd care for her. I need your help."

More than anything, Esther wanted to cry or maybe scream. More than anything, she wanted to help Dan, relieve him of this one small problem. But to actually hold and touch and care for this baby, this baby that wasn't Donny, was asking too much.

Still, with trembling hands she reached for the bundle in Dan's arms—reached, then jerked away, then reached again with sheer determination.

Esther took the baby in her arms. Its face was filthy. Fine curls were coated with dirt and patches of mud. Even so, the angelic expression on the baby's face, the long eyelashes, and pudgy nose touched Esther. While something hard and hurtful melted away inside her, Esther could hardly hear Dan as he told her, "I have to go, Esther. Let Addy help you."

When next Esther looked up, she was aware that Dan had kissed her cheek because it was still warm, but he was driving off in the Bronco.

"Dan," she called.

Dan stopped and opened the crack in the window a little wider.

"A name. What's her name?"

"Susie."

Esther nodded, and Dan, apparently thinking the discussion was over or thinking of something else entirely, drove away once more.

"I love you," Esther said, knowing he hadn't heard her, hoping he knew she'd said it.

Susie slept through most of the night. Esther barely closed her eyes. Anxious and frightened, she sat and watched the child's body move with her respiration, listened for each breath, jumped nervously when she stirred.

She hovered over the child throughout the night, terrified that in the blink of an eye the baby would be gone—just like before. Minute by minute the child's survival became more and more vital to Esther. Deep-seated dreams, desires, and hopes staked themselves into the life of this stranger's child.

When at last Susie began to whimper and cry, becoming restless as she woke, Esther was close beside her. Bright blue eyes opened sleepily, eyes that were so different from Donny's in color, and yet so similar in their innocence and trust.

Esther smiled her reassurance to Susie and gently stroked the top of her dry, mud-soaked head. Willingly, the child moved into Esther's arms and was held safe and protected.

Esther's heart overflowed with emotion for Susie, for her spirit and her future. New life rose within her, filling her with desire and a need she thought had been destroyed forever.

She fairly floated as she picked up Susie and started for the kitchen.

"Your tummy is going to be a ball of pain pretty soon. Let's get you some milk to keep it quiet, while I fix you some real food, huh?" Esther said brightly. "Then I'm going to bathe you till you shine again, you muddy little mess."

Opening the refrigerator, she brought out the milk.

"Then we'll play until Mommy and Daddy come to get you," Esther promised Susie, refusing to think it would be any other way.

Susie was impatient while the milk warmed. Her crying brought a grumpy Addy to the kitchen door.

"Hell's bells, child, turn the fire up under that stuff and feed her. She's loud enough to wake the dead," Addy complained. "She must be feelin' better, huh?"

"Seems to be," Esther agreed. "Do you suppose Dan would be upset if I called to check on her father?"

"No. He's a good man. Told you so when you first come back. He'll understand your worry."

First things first, Esther decided as she made oatmeal with honey and fed Susie until the baby turned her face away and refused to open her mouth again.

Next on the list was a much-needed bath, but talking to Dan took priority.

Miles away, Dan was up to his old tricks. Reading her mind, knowing she'd be concerned, Dan called Esther just as she was reaching for the phone.

"Hi, sweetheart. Are you all right?" he asked.

"Yes. What about you? How did it go? How are you feeling? I've been worried about you."

She heard Dan laugh and instantly felt better.

"My hands took over like they were on automatic pilot. It went well. He'll be fine. How is the baby?" he asked, actually as curious about Esther's response as the child's condition.

He'd known all night that Susie was well, or Esther would have called him. What he really wanted to know he'd hear in Esther's voice.

"She's fine and cute as can be. I was just getting ready to bathe her and see what color her hair really is. She ate a truckload of oatmeal. I don't see how she can still move," Esther said enthusiastically.

Her words warmed Dan's heart with renewed love for her and the hope for babies of their own. "Enjoy yourself, Esther."

"I am. I really am."

"I know," Dan said thickly. "But don't get too attached. Her mother will be here soon to pick her up."

"Oh, Dan. Thank God," Esther uttered as tiny little chills of relief and joy spread through her. "Is she okay?"

"Yes. The day before yesterday she'd gone to Buckton to visit her mother. She couldn't get back over the bridge. We've called her, and the police will bring her over in a helicopter later today."

Dan went on to say that he wanted to stay a little longer with his patient but that he'd be home around lunchtime to shower and eat.

"Did you get any sleep last night?" Esther asked, concerned.

"I tried, but I missed you. I sat awake all night pining for you."

"Ha. Give me a break. You were down there playing hotshot surgeon and loving it. Admit it," Esther said lightheartedly.

"Okay. I admit it. It felt good to be doing what I do best again. But that doesn't mean I want a steady diet of it."

Esther felt it best not to push him on the subject. He already had Fesstus working on him; he didn't need her too.

"Is Eddy still with you?"

"No. Tom came barreling through here last night wanting to know where the hell he'd been all day."

What did Eddy say?"

"Not much."

"I probably shouldn't let him come here," Esther said, knowing it was worth the risk for her but wondering if it was the same for Eddy.

"I doubt you could stop him. He thinks you're pretty terrific. So do I, as a matter of fact."

Esther sighed her indecision.

"I love you," she said.

"I love you too. I'll be home later. Get some rest," he said, and finally hung up.

Esther knew her relationship with Eddy would have to be made public soon. His sneaking around to see her wasn't right, especially given the light under which his parents viewed Esther. Inevitably she and Eddy would have to have a showdown with Tom and Jewel.

However, Esther was afraid that poor Eddy would wind up getting the worst of it when all was said and done.

For now, however, the Belldons would have to be placed on the back burner. There was a baby waiting for her bath and Esther's fingers itched to get started.

She laughed at her maternal instincts that were bouncing out of control after such a long confinement. But she truly was enjoying herself. She had forgotten how soft and warm a baby's body could be. She had forgotten the sweet and unique baby smell that no manufacturer had ever been able to bottle. And she most certainly had forgotten how busy pudgy baby fingers could get.

The rest of the morning was spent moving Dan's possessions out of harm's way. More to the point, out of Susie's way. It soon became apparent that Susie was no baby, but a toddler with a very distinctive style and grace.

"I swear that child is going to knock herself out," Addy declared while she and Esther watched Susie careening from one piece of furniture to the next.

"No. Donny . . . Donny moved the same way for weeks. I think it's normal at first," Esther recalled, feeling a deep pain that she knew would remain with her always. But that was all she felt. The raw agony she had carried for so long had dissipated during the night, replaced by a sore, lonely ache.

Susie was asleep when Dan made it home. They stood by Esther's bed, which had been moved against the wall and lined with high-backed chairs, watching the small girl sleep.

"Her dad sends his thanks," Dan told Esther in a whisper.

Esther only nodded acknowledgment.

"Esther. Are you all right, sweetheart?" Dan asked.

Esther sensed that he knew her pain, her thoughts and every emotion from the tone of his voice and the pressure of his arm as it curled around her shoulders lovingly.

She nodded once again as emotion and instinctive need shook her. Stepping forward, she wrapped Dan's arms about her from behind and pressed back into him.

"Dan. Will you give me a baby? I want another baby. Our baby," she said around the lump of desire in her throat.

"Whenever you're ready," he promised, kissing her just below her earlobe. "How about a little girl like Susie?

Esther agreed. "With your dark eyes."

"And your long black hair," Dan added.

Turning in Dan's arms, Esther wrapped hers around his neck. "I'm going to tell her every day that I love her."

Dan was sure she would. She'd never take a child for granted, but would consider it a precious gift. She'd make sure her children knew they were loved and cherished.

"What about me?" Dan asked, screwing his face up pitifully.

"I'll tell you twice a day," she whispered.

"And I'll be glad to hear it, happier when you show me."

Dan's hands moved to the top button of Esther's blouse. The breathless anticipation of all she knew could happen when he touched her tingled in waves across her skin. Glancing over her shoulder at the sleeping Susie, Esther turned back to Dan, merriment twinkling in her eyes.

"It is naptime. I suppose we should take advantage of that fact," Esther said whimsically.

"I suppose we should."

"What about Addy?"

"She said to call if you needed her and left when I came in."

"How astute of her," Esther said.

"Well, she also said something about recognizing a certain look in my eye," Dan said, grinning, as he pulled Esther out of the room by the shirtfront that was still in his hands.

"You know, if we observe naptime when we have our own children, I'll bet we could get in three, maybe four lovings a day," he stated, inspired.

Esther laughed and watched him come toward her with a look of gentle tenderness and caring in his eyes, devilish humor dancing around his lips.

"Think you can handle all that loving?" Esther asked, a slow, taunting smile curving her own lips.

She watched as Dan's talented fingers took up their work on her buttons.

"Can you handle cocky as opposed to just confident?"

"I think so," she replied.

"Then so do I."

Dan lowered his head to place kisses in the hollow of her neck, even as his hands peeled the blouse away from her skin.

Nine

Later in the afternoon the sheriff drove up in front of the house. Esther knew, without looking to see, that Susie's mother had come for her baby.

All at once she was happy and sad and angry and jealous and grateful. She wasn't sure how to feel or what to do first. That both of the baby's parents were well and safe, and that Susie's story would have a happy ending filled Esther with relief and gladness for them all. But she also didn't want to give Susie back.

Esther bent to pick up the little girl while Dan opened the front door and walked out onto the porch. She could hear voices outside as she straightened Susie's soft blond hair into place, trying to memorize the wondrous feeling of having a baby in her arms again.

Dan reentered the house, watching Esther's face with concern as he held the door open behind him. A young blond woman followed him in. Her tired, worried expression brightened like a thousand neon lights when she saw Susie.

"Susie. Baby," the woman gasped, racing forward.

Suddenly the mother stopped and looked at Esther

anxiously. It then occurred to Esther that she was probably looking very protective and possessive of Susie—that was how she felt. Reluctantly Esther handed Susie to her mother.

"Thank you so much for taking care of Susie. When Doc told me she was in the most loving hands he knew of . . . well, I felt a lot better. Thank you," Susie's mother said in a most heartfelt way. She held her daughter tightly, cuddling her closely.

"It was a pleasure. I'm glad I could help," Esther said. "If . . . if you need someone to watch her while your husband—"

"Oh, thanks," the woman interrupted gratefully. "But the sheriff has made plans to take us back to my mama's house."

"I'm glad things turned out as well as they did for you."

"Oh. Me too. We only lost things. When I think of what I coulda lost, I feel real lucky," she said.

The young mother had eyes very like her daughter's. Looking at them, Esther could see they belonged together. Heartsick, she forced herself to let go of Susie.

Dan performed the rest of the amenities, and when the sheriff's car drove away, he was already halfway across the room to take her in his arms. He held her quietly for a long time, enjoying the feel of her, letting her take from him whatever she needed.

"So. Do you want this black-haired, black-eyed baby girl before or after we get married?" he asked, his tone lightly teasing.

"I'm not looking to pass on my title," she answered against his warm, soft flannel shirt.

"Your title?"

"They used to call me the 'Bastard of Bellewood.'"

Dan sighed heavily, cursing her memories and his stupidity. "When can we get married, then?" he asked, perfectly serious.

Esther looked up into Dan's deep, solemn eyes. She saw the tenderness in his expression and knew her life was bound to his whether they married or not. More than a baby, more than her music, she wanted this man.

"Soon. After everything settles down. We still have some things to work out."

"Like?"

"Like I can't live here forever. It's not as bad as I remembered it, but I still can't stay here."

"I know. I was wondering when you'd start talking about leaving again."

"Can you leave? Will you leave with me?"

"Do you want to go back to California?"

"No. Not necessarily," Esther said, then considered, "I think I could swing being a surgeon's wife in D.C."

She felt him tense in her arms, but he didn't move away. He was still listening, still willing to talk about it.

"At least try it, Dan. You're wiser now. It won't swallow you up again. You were young, ambitious, and idealistic. It didn't gobble you up, you jumped in and buried yourself in it. You couldn't have been prepared for what it would be like. I'm sure they don't teach basic gore and horror in med school." Esther paused to take a breath. In a low, confident voice, she added, "You can do it, Dan. I know you can. You should at least give it one more chance."

Dan studied her face for a long, long time. Where did her belief in him come from? How could she be so certain about his abilities? What if he failed again? Could he stand the disappointment he'd see in her eyes?

"Do you need to leave right away?" he asked quietly.

"No. Of course not. But we should think about it."

"Then give me a little more time, okay?"

"All you need," Esther assured him, suddenly feeling distant from him.

Dan appeared to withdraw into himself. He was quieter than usual and monosyllabic—it frightened Esther. Had she pushed him too hard? Would he force her to choose between him and Bellewood? Would he waste his life and talents here, always yearning to do what he was meant to do because he was afraid to try?

And who was she to advise him? At least he could verbalize his fears, while hers stayed inside to fester. What would Dan think of her faith in him if he knew she had no faith in herself?

Later in the afternoon and again after dinner Dan drove down to the clinic to check on his patient. He returned late to find Esther asleep in a chair.

Both were exhausted from the strains of the last forty-eight hours, both were tired of talking, debating, even thinking about their fears and inner turmoil. They went to bed. With legs intertwined and Esther's head resting over Dan's heart, she listened to the strong, steady rhythm as it lulled her into a deep slumber.

The rain had finally stopped, but it was another two days before the flood waters began to recede. At first in small groups, and then later as neighbors joined in, the homeless victims of the flood began to pick up their lives again.

As each foot of water moved away from the land, the people of Bellewood advanced. From the mud and debris they salvaged what was left of their homes. Faced with their losses, the shock of the disaster wearing off rapidly, it became increasingly hard to remember to be grateful that not a single life had been lost. Instead their thoughts turned to the cost of new homes and the loss of personal possessions that were irreplaceable.

Esther had to admire them. Mourning their losses was a natural and understandable thing to do. But there was never any question about their starting over. Life would go on. They would begin again and rebuild their homes. Together neighbors and victims alike would readjust their lives, work harder than usual, and return to normal daily living, almost as if the flood had never happened.

Hoping that the feeling of acceptance she had experienced the night of the flood wasn't all part of the numbness induced by the emotional aftermath of the flood, Esther joined in the recovery. She found she had an endless supply of energy and goodwill when the people of Bellewood accepted her help without bias. They worked beside her and included her in their discussions. They acknowledged her opinions and ideas on the basis of their merit, and at the end of the day she was included in the generalized but heartfelt appreciation.

A sense of purpose and usefulness filled Esther. It was a feeling she'd always enjoyed but hadn't felt much of lately. While she labored along the riverbanks focusing her thoughts on someone else's problems, her own dilemmas and insecurities were easily forgotten.

Nearly a week and a half had passed since the flooding. The late April days alternated between sunny pleasant weather and drizzling overcast conditions that made their work even more depressing. It was on one of the sunnier days, however, that Dan found time to join Esther at the river.

There had actually been many such days, when Dan would find his medical duties completed and several free hours available to work on a cleanup project. He almost always made a point of seeking Esther out and working alongside her. No longer concerned that she might have a relapse or that she wasn't strong enough to help, Dan sought Esther's workingplace simply to be with her. He enjoyed looking at her.

Esther was glad to see him. Catching sight of the Bronco or of Dan himself walking toward her always set her heart a-flutter. Tall, lean, and broad-shouldered in jeans and a flannel shirt, Esther knew her spine grew several inches higher with pride when he placed a public kiss of greeting on her lips before going to work with the others.

She found herself looking forward to sunny days when Dan would become overheated and remove his shirt. Esther enjoyed watching his muscles ripple beneath his white T-shirt while he labored effortlessly. And there was definitely something very arousing in the display of his superior physical strength.

"Where can I start?" Dan asked, hanging a proprietary arm across Esther's shoulder after he'd kissed her hello. "And have I told you lately how cute you look with mud on your nose?"

Wearing rubber boots to mid-calf, jeans, and one of Dan's old flannel shirts over her own cotton blouse, Esther was sure her nose wasn't the only place where she was covered with mud. Taking a swipe at her face with the sleeve of her shirt, she looked up to Dan for his inspection.

"Better?"

"What would your fans say if they could see you now?" he asked as he meticulously removed the rest of the offending dirt with his finger.

"You're my biggest fan. What do you think?"

"I told you. I think it becomes you. So do those roses in your cheeks and the healthy glow in your eyes," he said, moving with his gaze to each part of her face as he spoke about it.

"Ya done good work, Doc," Esther said, grinning. "But am I still too skinny?"

Dan ran his free hand up and down her ribs between her breasts and hip very slowly.

"Maybe just a little, but it's a vast improvement over the bag of bones you were in February," he said, eyes twinkling.

"Bag of bones!" Esther exclaimed, laughing. "Look, buster, I'll have you know that—"

Dan placed a single finger to her lips to silence her.

"And I'll have you know I really don't care how fat or skinny you are as long as you're healthy and happy."

"Yeah? Well . . . okay," Esther said, backing down a little.

He kissed her quickly on the forehead.

"Cliff looks like he could use some help over there," he said, looking over her shoulder. "I'll see you later."

Dan walked away from her, but she could hear his mumbling. "And don't you give a second thought to the fact that I prefer meaty women in bed. . . ."

"Hey!" Esther called to his back.

Dan turned to her, grinning mischievously, and winked. Then he went about his business as if he didn't know he'd planted a seed of desire in Esther, or that it would grow rapidly throughout the afternoon as she caught glimpses of him toiling with the other men of Bellewood.

The Peterson home had been totally destroyed in the flood. It had fallen into a heap of rubble, bits and pieces of it breaking away and floating downstream. The men had moved in as soon as the water had receded, removing much of the lumber and other remains by hand or with forklifts and dump trucks. Afterward, the area was safe for the Petersons, three of their children, and some of their neighbors to scrounge through the sludge and rubble left behind for anything salvageable.

Esther had joined Dotty Peterson in the cool of the morning. Dan had arrived shortly after noon. They filled a Super Red Flyer wagon full to overflowing with pots and pans, figurines, soggy blankets that might wash clean, cups, glasses, and a multitude of other household goods to be cleaned and stored at a neighbor's house.

Esther was making her fifth trip of the day up River

Street with her little red wagon full of buried treasures when she first heard Eddy coming into town. He neither waved nor signaled in her direction, but she intuitively knew he was coming to see her. Dread spread through her veins. Up until now all their meetings, their friendship, and subsequent relationship had been retained within the walls of Dan's house. A public meeting could and very likely would precipitate the scene she had been trying to avoid for seventeen years.

Not that she'd always wanted to elude this particular skirmish, she realized. For years she had planned and fantasized about the battle and defeat of the precious Belldon family name. But with time, the shame and pain had ebbed. Confidence and a sense of self-worth dulled the hatred, and with maturity Esther found great pity for the small, hurtful minds she'd left behind in the hills of West Virginia.

As she had told Dan, she would no longer draw pleasure from destroying the lives of those who had made her life so miserable. But she also would no longer avoid it if confronted—and meeting Eddy in public would most certainly increase the odds of just such a confrontation.

Esther stopped. Glancing around, she saw no one within hearing distance and decided if she was going to talk to Eddy, she preferred to be seen doing so but not heard.

Eddy pulled up beside her. "Hi, Auntie Esther," he said, taking off his helmet to show his teasing smirk.

"I thought I warned you about calling me that in public," she said, not bothering to hide her displeasure.

"You did. But I don't care if people know we're related. I'm proud of it," Eddy said defensively.

"I'm glad, but try to remember your dad might not be."

Eddy made a disrespectful and uncaring grimace.

"I'm not kidding, Eddy," Esther said firmly. "He's been cruising through here off and on every day since the flood. If he saw you talking to me, he'd come unglued."

"That's not fair," the boy complained. "I've got rights too. I should be able to talk to anyone I want. Including my own aunt."

"Right, Eddy," Esther agreed scornfully. "That sounds pretty good on the pages of a history book, but are you willing to teach this lesson to your dad? Because I'm not crazy about the idea myself."

"How come you're mad at me? My dad's the one who doesn't like you. You could tell him who you are. Maybe you could be friends," the boy said hopefully but didn't really sound convinced.

"I'd rather let sleeping dogs lie, Eddy. Dragging up the past will only be painful for all of us. Your dad has been pretty good about staying out of my way while I've been here. I'd be smart to do the same."

"Fine. Great," Eddy said angrily. "And what about me? Is it over between us too?"

"You whore!" an hysterically angry voice shouted from behind them. Both Esther and Eddy turned to see Jewel Belldon closing in on them with a vengeance.

Esther had seen that same look in her eyes before. Fear and panic engulfed her automatically, like a childhood reflex.

"I should have guessed," Jewel said with a hiss between clenched teeth. "All your money hasn't changed you a bit. You're still the whore's daughter, aren't you?"

"Mom," Eddy said, horrified by his mother's actions.

"Stay out of this, Edgar, you have no idea what she is," Jewel ordered.

As if taking off a pair of sunglasses, everything suddenly became clear and calm to Esther. She had nothing and no one to fear here anymore. She wasn't a child who could be beaten with fists or cut with words anymore. She knew the truth of who and what she was, and it had nothing to do with the presence or absence of a father.

Jewel Belldon was a stupid, bitter, lonely, and insecure woman. Esther felt very sorry for her.

Eddy looked frightened by his mother's behavior. His hands were fidgeting on the bars of his bike, and he couldn't meet either woman's gaze.

Over Jewel's shoulder Esther could see Dan covering the distance between them with long, purposeful strides. Some of the other workers followed him. Esther's heart was growing heavy in her chest. Not only was she going to have to fight Jewel, but now they'd have an audience.

She had time only to half-wish that Dan would stay away and encourage the others to do so as well before she spotted the reason for his determined pace. A black Continental had turned onto River Street and was bearing down on them.

Esther sighed and let her eyes close fatalistically. More than anything, she wanted to try to remember how much more she'd gotten in life than Tom and Jewel Belldon had. She wanted to remain calm and kind. She held all the cards this time, but she didn't have to use them, did she?

Esther wanted to be forgiving, but she could feel that sixteen-year-old girl within her, raising her fists once more, spreading her legs for balance, preparing to fight if she had to.

"I know what you're up to, Esther Brite," Jewel turned to attack. "You couldn't seduce Tom as a girl, so you've come back to take your revenge on his son. He's only sixteen. I'll have you arrested. Tom should have run you out of town when you first got here, like I told him to. We can get another doctor. They're a dime a dozen."

"What are you talking about?" Esther finally asked.

"I'm talking about you, you stupid slut."

"What were you saying about Dan?" Esther asked as Dan stopped beside her, his breath ragged and rapid.

"Oh, isn't this cute," Jewel said with a simpering

smile. "Come to defend your little rock 'n' roll star, Doctor?"

"Look, Mrs. Belldon," Dan started to say, but Esther finished for him: "Leave him out of it, Jewel."

"Ha! He told Tom if we forced you to leave town, he'd go with you. Seems to me he's in this up to his . . . well, just how far have you gotten with him, Esther?" Jewel's voice was taunting.

No one answered Jewel as their attention was drawn to the elegant black car pulling up to them. A fairly large crowd had gathered by now, and a certain tension seemed to ripple through it as Tom Belldon got out of the car.

"What the hell is happening here?" he asked. His gaze went directly to Esther for an answer.

"A lot you care. If you'd done what I told you to when she got here, this wouldn't have happened," Jewel told him.

"What?" Tom asked pointedly of Jewel, as if she were his village idiot.

"I caught this whore trying to seduce Edgar. Something's been going on, because I heard him asking if it was finished between them," Jewel told him venomously.

Tom looked dubious for a second, and then a strange expression crossed his face. The silence grew ominous as he raked his gaze over Esther. When he finally spoke, it was in a tone of voice that Esther recalled vividly. It was the voice of a mean, angry boy.

"Tell me, boy, is she still the best lay in Bellewood?"

Instantly Esther felt Dan move at her side and she threw her arm up in front of him to stop him. Her gaze, however, was riveted on Eddy.

She had been expecting Tom's foul nastiness, and even though her muscles tensed angrily, she wasn't as outraged as she should have been. Instead, she watched as Eddy took on her injury and grew defensive.

"Esther isn't like that, Dad," he said vehemently. 'Not now and not back then."

"Is that right?" Tom questioned with a knowing laugh.

"Yes, that's right. She's been nothin' but nice to me, and I like her."

"I'll bet." Tom laughed again as if he knew exactly what his son meant. Jewel gasped indignantly.

Dan muttered something and pushed against Esther's arm with such force that she had to turn and place both hands on his chest to prevent him from attacking Tom.

"Please," Esther whispered up to Dan. "I'll help Eddy if he needs it. We can handle this. Please."

Dan looked fierce, but he backed off slightly to give her a chance.

"You're making a big mistake here, Dad. I'm the one who went to see Esther. She didn't ask me to come, I just went. We never did anything wrong. We talked. She's nice. She's my friend."

"She's everybody's friend, boy," Tom informed Eddy with great wisdom.

"No, she isn't. She's your sister," Eddy blurted out in rage and frustration.

"Like hell!" Tom bellowed, crossing his arms defensively across his chest. He looked like a man standing in the middle of the road. He knew the Mack truck was coming but didn't move. He just stood there, hoping it wouldn't hit him.

"It's true, Dad. Tell him, Esther," Eddy pleaded.

"I don't think I need to," Esther said quietly. "I think he knows, or at least he's suspected it. Am I right, Tom?"

Fury and resentment narrowed Tom Belldon's eyes. His jaw was set firmly. Esther got the impression that killing her, eliminating her from his life once and for all, was not far from his mind. Her heart hammered rapidly. The palms of her hands grew moist while she waited for his response.

The crowd began to talk. People mumbled under their breath to one another. Esther had an insane urge to laugh. It seemed ironic that it would take them over thirty years to finally start putting the pieces together, to begin noticing the physical similarities between Tom Belldon and Esther Brite.

Tom apparently was going to refuse to admit or deny his suspicions. He stood seething silently, daring Esther to prove herself.

"How else would someone like my mother get a job in the office? How could she afford to own her own home? If your mother were still alive, she could tell you. She could tell you how she paid me to leave town after our father died. She could tell you how she promised to provide for my mother if I left town. And how she threatened to destroy her, leave her jobless and destitute, if I didn't go."

The crowd rumbled a little louder, and Tom grew florid with rage and hatred.

"Your mother was a whore," he shouted at last, unable to keep it inside any longer.

"Yes, she was. And our father slept with her," Esther said simply, feeling no need to deny the facts any longer.

"They used to fight about you all the time," Tom said with bitter resentment. "I never knew the real reason, but you and your mother were always at the heart of it. She'd barb him with little comments about you, and he'd get madder 'n hell. *I* could never do *anything* right, but he'd sure as hell go to bat for a couple of cheap prostitutes. . . . I hated your guts."

The force of his words hit Esther. Something inside her twisted and ached terribly. His loathing was as tangible as Dan's hand on her shoulder. It was one thing to know someone hated you but quite another to have them tell you so with such passion and violence. In disbelief Esther felt her heart reaching out to him. Having learned to pity him for his bigotry and cruelty, she found empathy for his own miserable childhood.

"It was all your fault. Your mother didn't deserve a real job. Mother said they practically had to teach her how to read and write when she started, and you . . . you with your high and mighty attitude of being as good as the rest of us. Neither one of you knew your place. A whore and her bastard pretending to be real people."

Suddenly Esther realized he resented not only what she was, but who she had become as well. The father-less girl deserved no more than the life from which she'd come. For her to become rich, famous, and suc-cessful was revolting to Tom. It didn't fit into his sense of fairness. Or was there more to it? Had Tom himself aspired to leave Bellewood only to find himself tied to the mines? As a boy had he been similar to his son, Eddy, who had had great dreams and ambitions of being something other than the owner of the Bellewood mines?

Jewel, who had been silently standing by absorbing the facts, enjoying what she thought was a humiliating experience for both her husband of too many years and his half sister, finally felt compelled to speak her piece.

"You're disgusting, Esther. All those years of throw-ing yourself at Tom. Taunting him and encouraging him to chase you around. And all along he was actually your brother. Really, it's just too . . ."

"Shut up, Jewel," Tom said stingingly. "As usual, you don't know what you're talking about."

"Yes. I do," she insisted. "I was in love with you. I saw the way you watched her. I was glad when she left. You were angry. I've always come in second."

Tom stood staring at his wife as if she were speaking Greek. Minutes passed as a frown creased his brow. His thoughts were indecipherable as the crowd and Esther stood tensely by awaiting his next response.

At last his gaze lowered from his wife's face and he looked out toward the mountains and the mines. When he again turned back, his gaze fell on Esther.

She saw a tired, beaten man who expected her to kick him while he was down. That it was her move to perhaps reveal his wickedness to the world or to use her knowledge to make a play for at least half of what filled his life was all too evident as he stood waiting for her to speak.

"I can see we've hurt each other a lot over the years," Esther started cautiously. "It's kind of a shame we ended up paying for a mistake we didn't make."

Esther was extremely nervous. She wasn't at all sure that what she was about to do was what she really wanted to do. Nevertheless, the desire to do it was there. Now was the time to put the question to sleep forever.

"I don't suppose we could try to start over." She didn't sound too optimistic herself. "There's just the two of us left. It might be worthwhile. . . ."

Esther slowly stopped speaking as Tom shook his head. She saw that he had begun to rub the scar on his wrist as if it were paining him.

"Too late," he said firmly. "It's been too long. Too much has happened."

Esther nodded her understanding, accepting his decision, feeling only disappointment and regret.

"What about Eddy?" she asked. "We've become friends, and I swear I'd never hurt him in any way."

Tom considered her statement, then turned to look at his son. Eddy didn't say a word, but his plea and the trust he held in his father's better judgement were written on his face.

"He's a big boy. He can do as he pleases," Tom conceded, neither encouraging nor discouraging Eddy's relationship with Esther.

"Tom! She's a—" Jewel started to protest in horror before she saw the quailing expression on Tom's face.

Without another word he took his wife's arm and led her back through the crowd to his car, where he opened the door and assisted her in. Taking one last look at Esther and apparently deciding his decision was the right one, he got in and drove away.

Knowing Dan was behind her, ready to catch or defend her as needed, Esther leaned back into his comfort and strength as the tension drained quickly away from her.

Dan wrapped his arms around her. He placed warm, loving kisses on her temple. In a voice cracking with his devotion and admiration, he asked, "You all right, honey?"

Esther nodded numbly. The battle instigated at her conception was finally over. There had been no victory or defeat. There had been no winner or loser or resolution, but it was over nonetheless. There would never be a need to reenact it, because already, before the echo of the words had died away, it was in the past.

Ten

According to Esther's agent, time was passing. But on a warm, lazy Saturday afternoon in May, who cared? She lay in the sun watching tall, tufted clouds tumbling in the blue sky above her. The delirious singing and chirping of birds filled her ears. The sweet smell of honeysuckle came to her on the occasional light breeze. And she knew she had only to adjust her vision slightly to see Dan, her prinicpal source of happiness, vigorously washing and cleaning her little red car . . . with his shirt off.

She knew that a truly wise person would embrace the tranquillity of the day. She'd count her blessings and know in her heart that life just didn't get any better than this. A smart person would know that health and love were unpurchasable. She'd lay in the sun, warm and contented.

Part of Esther was very wise, very smart. Part of her asked for nothing more, except perhaps a baby someday. That part of her was amazed she could have ever found such contentment in Bellewood.

However, Esther was only human. Another part of

her was greedy, selfish, and discontented. She had an almost neurotic compulsion to make music, to put her emotions into words and melodies. She missed the sense of purpose in her life, missed the fame and recognition of her talents. But what had been so easy before, what had come so naturally for so long, was no more. Her heart, although full to overflowing, was silent. No music or words burst forth in her happiness. They lay trapped in her soul, unable to vent themselves.

Esther sighed her frustration and sadness. If only she'd become famous on her own in the first place without Seth, she'd know now she could do it again. But Seth had been so dynamic, it was hard to tell in retrospect if her songs had actually made all that much difference. Would he have made it to the top singing someone else's songs? Or was it the combination of her music and his talent that had brought them success? Would her songs, written for others to sing, be as popular or well-received as the songs she had written for Seth? Lord, at this point, she'd be glad just to write a jingle. She didn't even care if it was a good or bad jingle. It would be a start.

Again she released a long breath of malcontent. Surely there must be something else to occupy her mind besides the questions she'd been pondering for over a year now.

The day was so beautiful, the sun so warm, it was hard to believe the mess things had been in six weeks earlier. Nearly all of the flood ruins had been cleared away. The victims of the disaster were looking for new homes, and it was rumored that the company had no intentions of building any homes on the stretch of land near the river. If additional housing were found to be necessary, they would build elsewhere.

Dan's surgical patient was completely well now except for some additional healing time for one leg. Last week he and his wife had brought Susie to see Esther with a bouquet of flowers. It was a thank-you to her for caring for Susie in their absence. Esther had been touched by their gesture. There would always be a special place for Susie in her heart, because it was Susie who had shown her that her capacity to love transcended her pain. The fact that she could love another child gave Esther hope for one of her own someday, for which she would be eternally grateful.

Avidly avoiding her problems, Esther's thoughts drifted to Eddy, who continued to visit frequently. His parents were apparently making no effort at all to keep them apart.

"They never say anything about it one way or another," Eddy had said not long ago. "So I don't say anything either. They know I come here. We just don't discuss it." Then he'd added, "Actually, all they do seem to be talking about is that cruise they're going on. Jeez, you'd think they'd never been on a boat before."

Esther gave this some thought. "Have they?"

"I don't think so." Eddy grinned.

"Have you?"

"No." His grin widened sheepishly.

Eddy also was happier these days because his parents were no longer looking for another boarding school for him to attend.

"I guess they finally caught on that I don't want to go away to school yet," he'd said as he reached past Dan for another warm chocolate chip cookie that the two of them were eating as fast as Esther could bake them.

"But a boarding school might make it easier for you to get into college. Buckton is a pretty good school, but a prep school would have a better reputation," Esther said.

"I don't care about that stuff. I get good grades, and I'll do okay on the S.A.T.'s. That's all that counts."

"But—" she started, but Dan cut her off.

"There might be a more important reason for staying in Bellewood other than the curriculum over at Buckton," Dan said meaningfully.

Esther had frowned at them both in confusion. Until she spotted the look in Dan's eyes. A look Addy said could be spotted in a man a mile off. No expert in men in general, Esther had most assuredly come to know this particular look of Dan's.

Her simple "Oh" held a wealth of understanding.

Eddy wanted to stay in Bellewood because of a girl. Since that day, they'd been able only to drag out the girl's name, her general physical description, and even broader personality profile from Eddy. He was being very tightlipped about her.

Aw, puppy love, Esther thought as she sighed once again. If youth is wasted on the young, so be it, Esther decided. They deserve every minute of it.

Which brought her back to her agent. "Time's a-wastin', Esther," Max had told her that morning. "Even legends have to keep their names in the paper, or people forget all about them. I've had all sorts of people asking what you're planning to do with your music. It's time to let them know."

Esther had stalled for more time. Max made a living exerting pressure and keeping his clients productive. And every entertainer knew that agents have an exaggerated sense of time, always asking for more in less.

Still, it had been almost two years since Seth's death. The public had a short memory. A producer's recollection was even shorter.

Esther wanted to scream in hopelessness and defeat. Restlessly she flopped over onto her stomach. She was sick of blue skies and happiness. Sick of searching for music that wasn't there. Sick of people pressuring her to produce; sicker still of being unable to. Her brow furrowed, and tears welled in her eyes as she bit her quivering lip, refusing to cry. A fourth deep and ragged breath escaped her.

"You don't have allergies, do you?" Dan asked curiously as he finished buffing the wax off her car.

"No." But her throat and chest were tight with grief.

"Are you having trouble breathing? I've counted four huge sighs in the past fifteen minutes."

"No."

"Anything wrong?"

"No."

"Hungry?"

"No."

"Do you love me?"

Esther paused only an instant, then turned onto her side, supporting her head with her hand.

"I'm glad you didn't say no again," Dan said, grinning, knowing she loved him, not really needing to hear the words. "What's wrong?"

Esther smiled back. Dan would understand if she told him. He felt much the same way, except his talent was still there, still useful. He was just too wary to use it. In her heart she knew he would resolve his reluctance eventually. But would she?

"Nothing really," she said, her pride keeping her from telling him. Without her music she was ordinary—less than ordinary. There was nothing else about her that made her any more special than a zillion other women. And she wanted Dan to go on thinking she was special for as long as possible.

Dan took one final swipe at the gleaming red finish, then stood back to survey his work.

"Not bad, huh? Can't even tell it was an ornament for a mud pie for two weeks, can you?"

"Nope," Esther agreed as she watched his tall, lean, shirtless body move toward her. There was something so graceful and athletic, so strong and forceful about him that Esther never failed to feel her breath catch when he approached her. "You definitely have the hands of a healer."

Sitting on the blanket beside her, Dan said, "Cars don't respond the way people do. And I've never met anyone who responds to my hands the way you do."

To prove his point, Dan traced the scooped neck of

her tank top and ran a single feathery touch down her bare arm. Goose flesh followed in its path and Esther laughed.

"Are you aware that there are two flies fornicating on your leg?" he asked absently, moving his hand lower.

"Yes. They've been *bugging* me all afternoon."

Dan's response to Esther's pun was a deadpan expression and a long, suffering sigh, even as his eyes twinkled at her silliness.

"Okay. So, my sense of humor is warped. How's 'I got tired of waving them away and decided to ignore them'?"

"Better. But you never did answer my question," Dan said, but seemed far too absorbed with her bare thigh to care about her answer.

"Which question?"

"Do you love me?"

"Yes. You know I do," she said.

"Why won't you tell me what's wrong, then?" Dan asked. His gaze moved to hers, deep and probing.

He knew her so well and yet there were still thoughts he couldn't read, moods he couldn't decipher. He didn't mind that she had her private thoughts; she was entitled to them. But he knew she was worried about something and was deliberately shutting him out. He minded that a lot.

"There is nothing wrong. I'm just a little restless that's all," she said.

"Eager to leave Bellewood?"

Esther thought about the question. Would it help? No, she didn't think so. She felt very normal and uncluttered here. A bigger town and more pressure wouldn't help.

"No. Not really. Not this minute anyway. I think it's still spring fever," she said lightly.

Dan frowned.

"I thought we took care of that a while back," he said, sounding bewildered. "You seem to have a particularly bad case, Miss Brite."

"Oh, Dr. Jacobey," Esther whined playfully, grateful for the distraction from thinking about her turmoil. "You have no idea the pains I've been suffering. I do declare, I sometimes feel I may never recover."

"How terrible for you, Miss Brite. Let's see what we can do to relieve some of your discomfort, hmm?" He rose above her on one arm and gently pushed her back against the blanket. "Tell me your symptoms, please."

"I have some very disturbing butterflies in my stomach," she complained.

"It is that season," he said. He pulled the bottom of her tank top loose from her crisp shorts. Slipping a hand inside, he began to examine her abdomen in a most provocative way. "How they got in there is beyond me. I'm sure it's very disturbing. Tell me, is there anything else?"

"Just some buzzing in my ears."

"Must be a bee looking for a bird. Maybe I can blow the little bugger outta there for ya," he said with a straight face, his eyes dancing with delight. His head lowered to her ear. Dan began to blow gently and nibble on her lobe for good measure.

Little chills of ecstasy rippled through Esther's body. "Oh, Dr. Jacobey," Esther said with a gasp, not really pretending anymore. "I feel a sudden fluttering in my chest."

"Aw. The bee's bird," he exclaimed.

Quickly he straddled Esther's hips with his knees, effortlessly pulling off her top to expose her firm, peaked breasts to the heat of the sun and his hungry gaze.

"Let's have a listen here," he said facetiously, still playing the game Esther was quickly losing track of.

Cupping a breast in each hand, Dan lowered his head between them. He lay quietly listening while his thumbs worried and teased Esther's nipples into throbbing points.

"Poor little thing's knocking itself out in there," Dan said sympathetically.

"Mmm. I have a tingling in my lips, too, Doctor," Esther said, hoping Dan would treat this ailment as nicely as he had her others.

"Rub 'em together, Miss Brite. I'm a little busy right now." Then he opened his mouth over one aching breast and began to suck with an exact precision aimed to drive her insane with pleasure.

For Esther, the game was over. She allowed him to tend her other breast, then wove her fingers through his thick dark hair and took the kisses she was craving.

There on the blanket between the sun and the earth they joined in an act so pure and basic, so truly fine, they became part of nature itself. It was as if their hearts soared in the blue skies, their minds free-floated on a breeze of exquisite rapture, while their bodies became one with the rays of the sun.

"I hope you're listening for motorcycles," Esther mumbled against Dan's chest as they lay naked and satisfied on the blanket in Dan's front yard. She felt rather than heard his chuckle.

"Don't you think he'd laugh to see us streaking across the front yard into the house?"

"I just don't want him getting any ideas," she said.

Dan chuckled again.

"Esther, honey, he's sixteen years old. He already has ideas, lots of them."

Esther was thoughtful for a minute, then suggested, "When our little girl is sixteen, let's put her in a convent."

This time Dan laughed heartily, and rolling the two of them over, rose up to look down into Esther's eyes.

"No. I want our daughter to know the world. I want her to learn to be as strong and capable as her mother. I want her to be exposed to love and pain and joy. I want her to be as giving and forgiving as you are. She'll know these things only if you're there to teach her."

• • •

Several hours later Esther walked out onto the front porch of her childhood home and stared up at the stars. They seemed so far away, little pinheads of light so small she would be hard put to say if they were twinkling or not.

Jasper, making one of his rare social visits, must have sensed Esther's disquiet. The green-eyed cat moved out of the shadows to curl sympathetically around her legs. Not an overly affectionate animal, Jasper waited for his pat of gratitude, then moved away once more, leaving Esther alone with her thoughts.

Dan had helped her with the dinner dishes, then retired to his study to read. The piles of literature he read to keep up with his profession were staggering in Esther's estimation.

It also provided Esther with many an unoccupied evening such as this. Without Dan or Eddy to divert her, her mind became prey to all her doubts and apprehensions. Her body was tense and her nerves had once again reached the cracking point. She didn't need to replay the mental debate she'd fought so many times before to become weary and emotionally overwrought.

Dan was aware of Esther's restless prowling about the house. He heard the screen door close as she went out into the night. He frowned in concern. Her denials and feeble excuse this afternoon hadn't fooled him at all. Esther was deeply disturbed, and although she refused to share her anxiety with him, he was beginning to draw his own conclusions.

He knew for a fact that not a single score sheet had been removed from the box he'd given her in March. His instincts told him he'd win the bet if he wagered that she hadn't touched the piano in two months. Either he or Bellewood was stifling her creativity and she was suffering because of it.

He threw the journal he'd been reading into the cor-

ner and began pacing the room. It was all his fault.
Keeping her tied to Bellewood because of his cowardice
wasn't fair. She'd given so much of herself to him—her
love, her support, her encouragement—and all she got
in return were excuses and a plea for more time. She
empathized with the excuses and tried to hide the fact
that the time was killing her inside.

The thought brought back visions of their first days
together. The touch-and-go days in which Esther had
fought so hard to stay alive. If her spirit was as close to
death now as her body was then—the idea terrified
Dan.

He found himself at the screen door watching Esther
as she stood motionless in the dark. The enormity of
his love for her was so profound, it made his head reel
and his heart seem to burst wide open. The fact that
she loved him in return was a glorious and elating
feeling. He'd do whatever it took to make her happy.

Lost in her emotions, Esther heard the screen door
bump closed only seconds before she felt Dan's arms
around her. A sense of relief passed through her, eas-
ing some of her tension. In Dan she found solace and
comfort, he was her source of cheer. She took so much
from him, needed him so badly. He never pushed her
or made demands. He simply adored her and accepted
her love in return.

"Finished already?" she asked, leaning into him for
security.

He didn't answer, allowing her to think what she
liked. He pressed an affectionate kiss on her temple
instead.

"We need to talk, Esther," he said softly into her hair
as they stood looking out into the night.

"About what?"

"Your music," he stated directly.

In the time it took him to say the words, Esther's
defenses were in place. Her last haven from the pressure and confusion was now contaminated. Even Dan

was questioning her incompleteness. It wouldn't take him long to discover that her spirit had been shattered, her confidence mangled in the accident two years earlier.

"Let's not," she said hoping he'd back away and leave her alone.

"We need to, Esther. We need to get it out into the open and find a way to help you. I've seen how it's tearing you up inside. I want to help."

"You can't."

"I can try. We can find the problem and solve it together. Work something out," he said encouragingly, desperately.

"It's not something you can take a screwdriver to. You can't just tighten a few screws and make it like new, Dan."

"No. I know. But we can figure out what's wrong and change it. I think it's Bellewood and . . . me. If you need to leave Bellewood, we can. We can go anywhere you like. I'll start a new practice. I can work anywhere. Or if—if you need to be alone, away from me for a while, well, we can work that out too." He was silent for a moment, then added heartily, "Honey, I know how much your music means to you. It was there for you long before I was. I'd never be able to live with myself knowing I was keeping you from it."

Something inside Esther finally snapped. His readiness to sacrifice for her what he wouldn't do for himself was a massive, unwielding blow to her pride and self-respect. That he was willing to fight for something that no longer existed within her because she couldn't fight for it herself was so devastating, self-contempt overflowed and snapped her control in half.

In an agony of emotion she turned and lashed out at Dan. If he wanted to know how she felt, she'd show him. If he wanted to take her pain, she'd let him.

"Okay. All right. If you want to know what my problem is, I'll tell you. My music is gone. I'm so afraid I can't make it without Seth, I can't even hear it anymore. Not a note. Not a word. Nothing. I'm so full of fear, I've destroyed the only worthwhile thing about me, the only part of me that made me different from everyone else. What made me special. But you understand, don't you? You know as much about cowardice as I do, isn't that right? You're not keeping me from anything, Dan. So instead of probing my psyche and blaming yourself for my problems, which don't even involve you, why don't you heal thyself, physician. Why don't you take care of your own problems before you start meddling in mine."

The minute the words were out, echoing through the valley over and over again, Esther wanted to cut out her tongue. The look on Dan's face was a composite of shock and pain. His own torment and misery surfaced, exposing itself for more of her disapproval. And then it was gone. All of it. His expression was a mask of emptiness. There was no pain, anger, or shame. There was also no tenderness, understanding or love.

"Dan, I . . ." Esther verbally tried to reach out, to grab back her words, but it was too late. Dan pushed her hands away from him, turned his back to her, and went into the house.

What had she done? Destroyed the only thing in her life that meant anything, that meant more to her than her own life?

She heard the Bronco start up at the back of the house. Panic seized her. Where was he going? What was he going to do? How could she survive without him?

In a billow of dust the Bronco sped past the house toward the road.

"Dan," she called.

"Dan!" she screamed, but all that was left were two red taillights moving quickly away and the emptiness of the night, the emptiness of her life.

Racked with pain and tears, Esther held the porch

rail for support. Weak with defeat, she sank to her knees and let her sorrow have its way.

Esther sat up most of the night in an emotional abyss waiting for Dan to return. She wondered where he was, what he was doing, how he felt, and what would happen when he returned. She mentally flogged herself for being so selfish and cruel. In her fury and desire to punish her own weakness, she had only succeeded in hurting Dan and destroying the love and trust between them. Ironically she had delivered unto herself the ultimate penalty.

She must have fallen asleep for a time, because she came awake with a start to hear noises in Dan's bedroom. At the door she found a packed suitcase and on the bed two more to be filled. Dan's back was to her as he sorted through his closet choosing the possessions he'd be taking away with him.

"Dan. I'm sorry," Esther said in a voice laced with sorrow.

Dan turned to her then. For several seconds his deep, dark eyes were veiled and unreadable. Slowly understanding and tenderness softened his expression.

"I know you are, Esther," he said quietly.

"Can you ever forgive me? Can I make up for what I've done?"

Dan's smile was sweet and gentle.

"I know you were hurting last night. I've already forgiven you and there's nothing to make up for."

There it was. The ultimate rejection. Verbal noncommunication. Esther's heart constricted tightly, wringing out droplets of regret and despair.

"Oh, please, Dan. Don't do this. Don't shut me out. Please," she begged, moving several steps toward him. "I know I don't deserve your forgiveness and I . . ."

Dan walked swiftly across the room and took her by the forearms. In surprise, Esther fell silent.

"Listen to me, Esther," he said forcefully, his expression intent and impassioned. "I love you. More than anything else in the world. I'll always love you. What you said last night was the truth. How could I hate you for speaking the truth?"

He didn't really seem to want an answer, and as Esther had a feeling there was much, much more to come, she used her energy to brace herself instead.

"But I hope you remember what you said, because it was a truth for both of us. We've both been hiding out here, licking our wounds, fattening our insecurities with doubts and fear. And you were right. It's time for me to start living again, to face who I am and what I am and move on into the future. I'm going back to Washington and the trauma unit. I've got a second chance to make something of my life, and I'm going to take it."

Esther could feel his conviction and determination and knew he'd succeed this time. His patients would be individuals with unique pains and sufferings, and he would learn to walk the fine line between too much compassion and the callousness born in self-defense of taking on the anguish of others.

"I'm glad you've decided to do this," Esther told him, the pride in her face softening the lines of tension the previous night had induced. "If you give me a couple of minutes, I could pack and—"

Dan was shaking his head.

"No. I don't want you with me yet, Esther. I love you, and don't you forget it. But you still have your own little battle to fight, I think. The one you came here to fight in the first place. I don't want to pressure you or hinder you in any way . . . and I can't help you. You know that and I know it. The best thing for me to do now is to leave you alone to battle your own demon while I battle mine. When we're ready, we'll find each other again. We are meant to be together, but not right now."

Esther's lips moved to protest, but nothing came out. She had nothing to say. She wouldn't and couldn't hold him back. Nor would their life together ever be as glorious as it should be if they weren't both satisfied and in control of themselves.

His kiss was meant to last until the next one they shared. He held her close, avoiding the look on her face. The tears in her eyes were undermining his good judgment. He had to hold on to the belief that what he was doing was the best thing for both of them. He had to.

Dan had handled the situation as gently as possible, but it didn't save her any pain. She was still searching for a reason, any excuse to keep him close as she watched the Bronco fade out of sight. It was a bright, sunny May day, much like the day before, but she hardly noticed.

There was only one thought in her mind. It repeated itself over and over again. And it was too late to ask Dan about it. But . . . what if she failed? What if her music never returned?

Eleven

"Fesstus. You're impossible," Dan said under his breath to his favorite uncle. "And I'm an idiot for letting you talk me into this."

"Now, now," the old man said, "It's all part of the territory. You can't expect these fine people to part with their money if the trauma unit isn't properly represented."

"Wouldn't I be a better representative of what we do if I were performing surgery instead of just talking about it?" Dan asked.

"You wouldn't have time for a question and answer period," Fesstus said good-naturedly.

Dan released a resigned sigh. He didn't mean to be ill-tempered. He didn't want to be. But he couldn't seem to help himself. The only time he wasn't thinking and worrying about Esther was when he was elbow-deep in patients. Neither subject was conducive to cheerfulness.

For the first two weeks after he left, he'd been able to ease his mind about Esther with phone calls to Eddy. He hadn't wanted to cause her any extra grief by talking to her and having to say good-bye all over again. Eddy had been his easiest source of information.

Then, suddenly, she was gone. She'd told Eddy she had things to do and would be in touch. Her words to Addy had been much the same, with the added request of taking over the minimal care of Jasper. But where she was going and what she planned to do she kept to herself.

For eight months now there hadn't been a word written about her as far as Dan was able to ascertain. He was out of his mind with worry and concern about her, and he missed her more than he'd ever be able to say.

Leaving her alone might not have been as wise as he thought at the time. What if he'd left her when she'd needed him the most? The possibilities crossed his mind on an hourly basis.

Hope was all he had. Hope that Esther was safe somewhere, finding her way back to him. Hope that her quest was proving to be as easy as his had been.

He'd spent the first few months back catching up on the changes made in his absence. But his intuition and talent and skills proved to be in peak condition. It wasn't long before he settled into a comfortable routine, and the five years he'd been away almost forgotten. Almost.

He was very careful to protect himself against emotional overload. He found other things to occupy his mind in his off hours besides his patients. On the top of his list, of course, was Esther. Not on the list at all were elaborate fund-raising affairs for the trauma unit like the one Fesstus had dragged him to tonight.

The columned arcades and Great Hall of the historic Pension Building had been chosen to house this lavish affair. Hundreds of people were gathered. Celebrities, politicians, and wealthy citizens from all over the country had come to listen to Adair Delworthy sing and lend support to her cause. That her cause was also Dan's was a stroke of good fortune, but he still didn't want to be there.

Looking around, Dan decided the lime-green and pink walls he normally thought to be a hideous combination of colors didn't look too bad when softly lit and decorated in red and green for Christmas.

Only some of those attending had tables on the main floor, for which they'd paid large amounts of money to .eat a fairly simple meal. The two arcades above were now filling rapidly with people eager to hear Adair sing.

Dan slipped a finger inside his starched collar. Black formal wear was a far cry from the soft flannel he'd worn last Christmas.

Amazing how much could change in a year, he realized. He'd traded jeans and flannel shirts for suits and tuxedos. He'd come to terms with his fears and was doing the job he loved best. And his obsession with Esther had become a reality.

"So when does the fat lady sing? I want to go home," Dan asked uncomfortably.

"Adair Delworthy isn't fat," Fesstus said, knowing Dan had meant the expression to signify something else entirely. "And I'll have you know it was quite an accomplishment getting her to help us. The money she'll generate for the unit will close your mouth quick enough."

"How did you get her? Bashes like this are usually thrown for entire hospitals, not just one unit of it."

"She believes in the need for shock-trauma units. Part of our deal is to split the proceeds here tonight. Half for us and half to start another unit where it'll do some good," Fesstus explained.

Dan nodded. It was a good cause, he admitted to himself. And after all, it was only one night and the dinner hadn't been too bad. He should just sit back and enjoy listening to Adair Delworthy. He loved her music. How was Esther's doing, he wondered.

If Dan had known to wander backstage, he could

have had his answer firsthand. Esther, Fesstus, and Adair had been conspiring for months in preparation for this night. Actually, it had been Fesstus's idea, and Adair and her staff had done most of the work. All Esther had to do was be nervous.

"I'm so scared I think I'm going to die," Esther said to her friend Adair in the star's dressing room.

"Will you relax," the beautiful blonde replied. "You know the songs are good, or I wouldn't be using them on my next album. After all, I'm famous. I don't have to beg people for songs anymore. Actually, I think you should be ashamed of the way you made me beg for yours. We're supposed to be friends."

Esther smiled. She couldn't help but remember all the years she'd been friends with people and didn't even know it. Well, she'd known there were people whose company she preferred over others. She'd been aware that some of them had been very kind and friendly to her, asking for nothing in return. And she'd been careful to return their friendships, because she'd liked and admired them. But keeping so much of herself to herself for so long, she hadn't realy known they considered her a friend. She'd been stunned at her reception back into the musical fold—stunned and gratified beyond belief.

She'd spent those first couple of weeks in a daze, full of self-pity and reproach. Dan had arranged for a doctor from Westfield to come half-days until the company could replace him. He'd come to see Esther at Addy's request. His offer of a shot of B_{12} seemed ludicrous in light of her ailment. However, it was then she realized a shot in the derriere was exactly what she needed.

She'd left Bellewood several days later, determined to fight for what belonged to her. If her music never returned, it wouldn't be because she'd let it go in a pathetic, spiritless funk. She wouldn't cower in the face of her fears. She had to confront them, fight them.

And if she lost, it would have been a fair fight. At least, she'd have that satisfaction.

"If you ask me," Adair continued, "It's Dr. Jacobey you're nervous about. I swear, Esther, I'm proud to be a part of such a romantic event."

"I really appreciate all you've done."

"Hell, what I'll receive in publicity will more than make up for anything I've done."

"Two minutes, Miss Delworthy," a voice called through the closed door.

"This is it, Esther. Knock him dead."

Esther laughed nervously. "You too, Adair."

Standing in the darkened vestibule that was the entrance to the Great Hall, Esther was so anxious and distracted she wanted to cry . . . or laugh. She was trembling and clammy. Her arms and legs seemed to have a life of their own, and although she would have liked to appear the poised, confident artist everyone expected, she skittered around like a novice.

She'd decided to stake her whole future on one night. Her man and her music. She needed to hear an audience respond to her music. It didn't matter what agents and producers said. She needed to see and hear the people's reaction to her music. She'd know then if she could make it on her own talent. Without Seth's voice and charisma, her music would have to stand alone. Even though Adair was a superb singer, she was a breakaway from the past and could still be part of Esther's test.

And then there was Dan. All her phone calls to Fesstus had done little to relieve her worries about Dan. More than anything, she wanted to believe Fesstus when he said Dan was driving himself to distraction without her. It mattered little if Dan liked the music she'd written, only that he knew she'd written it, that she was whole again. But what she needed from this night was the look on Dan's face when he saw her. Then she'd know the last eight months and every month to come were worth living.

Listening to a brief warm-up by the orchestra, Esther reviewed the writing, orchestration, and rehearsing of her music. It had returned slowly. Her lyrics had been depressing enough to make a rock cry. The melodies that filtered into her consciousness sounded like sound tracks to Edgar Allan Poe movies. But it still qualified. It was music.

With renewed hope and the discovery and support of a network of friends she hadn't even realized existed, her music brightened. Like the water escaping the crack in the dam, the trickle became a torrent. The barrier holding back the musical expression of her emotions broke loose, flooding her mind and heart and soul.

Esther heard the familiar first strains of the song Adair was best known for as the star was announced. A thunderous round of applause rang out and Esther grew tense. She was in destiny's hands now. There was no turning back.

Adair was a performer from the word go. A true artist. Besides a clear voice, she had a style and manner that endeared her to fans all over the world. Esther had worn a strapless black sequined sheath gown and felt quite elegant, but next to Adair, who had worn white silk, she felt like a toad. For several seconds she let herself slip into the crowd and become part of them, enjoying Adair's special gift.

Two years had been a long time away from the entertainment world. She'd forgotten so much. Including how the adulation of a crowd at the end of a performance could sound. And how exciting yet sobering it could be.

Adair took it in stride. She seemed to anyway. She thanked the people for coming, for their generous contributions, and expressed her pleasure at being part of such a worthy cause.

Finally, Adair scanned the crowd until her gaze met Esther's. This was Esther's two-minute call.

"Tonight I also have the distinct honor and pleasure of welcoming back into the spotlight someone who has been sorely missed over the last couple of years. Recently this extremely talented composer and lyricist agreed to let me use several new pieces for an album. These are very special songs, and tonight before I bring our friend out here to take a bow . . . and to make her promise never to leave us again . . . I'd like to sing one or two of her wonderful new songs for you.

Adair's fans clapped encouragingly. She smiled thankfully, but held up her hand to stop them.

"Before I get started, though, I'd like to find someone in the audience, if I can," she said, carefully scrutinizing the tables on the main floor. "Is there a Dr. Daniel Jacobey from the trauma unit here tonight?"

From her vantage point, Esther couldn't see Dan, let alone the expression on his face. She did, however, see him when he stood and allowed the spotlight to find him. Even from behind, his dark head and tall, broad-shouldered figure dressed in black tripped Esther's heart into hyperspeed. Her throat was tight, her stomach alive with stage fright.

Esther hardly noticed the dazzling smile Adair flashed at Dan. She heard her announce Dan as the newly appointed chief surgeon of the trauma unit. The crowd gave him a round of applause. Esther could almost feel his self-consciousness. He sat down again but straightened when he saw Adair moving toward him, her hand outstretched.

Dan was surprised and flustered at having been singled out. There were other men present who were far more influential at the hospital than he. In truth, his title of chief surgeon was a pseudonym for paid slave, he thought, and carried only a limited amount of power in the overall scheme of things.

He, however, felt compelled to carry out what the

misinformed star had started. He met her halfway and
took her hand.

"Please, don't be uncomfortable, Doctor. But I was
told that right about now you'd either be asleep or
looking for a way to sneak out of here. I just wanted to
make sure you were still here and awake to hear these
songs."

"Why?" Dan asked, confused. His body was beginning to prickle with anticipation.

Adair gave him a Cheshire-cat smile and her eyes
twinkled at him merrily.

"Listen. Then wait and see."

Cautiously Dan returned to his place. He was positive it wasn't his birthday. So maybe whatever was
happening wouldn't be too humiliating. But something
was definitely happening. Intuitively Esther came to
mind once again. This was her music. She was here.
Frantically he searched what he could see of the backstage wings. He turned to Fesstus, who smiled inanely
at him. Dan was excited and impatient, ready to explode with expectation.

When the overture began, Esther left her hiding
place in the vestibule. She shook her hands to release some of the pent-up energy and breathed deeply
in and out through her nose, filling herself with
courage.

When Adair began to sing, Esther walked around the
tables, crossing the room, closing the distance between
her and the man she loved.

> There was a young girl deep inside me,
> Always longing to be free.
> She had hopes and dreams, ambitions.
> She knew the way things ought to be.
> I grew up, became a woman.
> Hid her drive, her strength, her charms.
> I put to sleep the girl inside me.
> But held her gently in my arms.

You fell in love with us.
Me, and the girl I used to be.
You believed in me and knew that she
Would be there in my need.

I followed life through destiny,
While the young girl slept in me.
She held the answers to my questions,
Knew what I needed to be me.
She held the hope to love again,
The faith to start anew,
The strength to see it through
And come back home to you.

Esther hardly heard the next chorus and verse. She stood within three feet of Dan, close enough to touch him, near enough to feel the heat his body generated, to sense his uneasiness as he listened to her words with rapt attention.

When the people around her recognized her and seemed inclined to approach her, she quickly smiled and raised her index finger to her lips. Letting them in on her surprise for Dan seemed the best way to avoid drawing attention to herself prematurely.

The song wound down, but before the last notes were being played out, Adair began to speak with great enthusiasm and pride.

"Please. Join with me in welcoming back the incomparable talent . . . Esther Brite!"

Esther felt the pull to acknowledge the crowd, but she kept her gaze riveted on Dan. The look on his face was most important to her.

With a jerking motion Dan turned in his chair. The dark eyes that met Esther's were filled with shock and disbelief, then with relief and happiness, and finally with abiding love and devotion.

"Esther," he whispered.

Esther smiled. But before she could speak, she was

in his arms. At first he simply held her tightly, possessively. Then he took her face in his hands, lifting it to
his. He searched it long and hard.

He looked as if he wanted to say so many things, but
all that came out was her name. It sounded like a
prayer.

Esther rose up and pressed her lips to his in a tender
expression of her own heartfelt emotions. As Dan deep-
ened their kiss, the clamor in her ears became a dull
roar that seemed to last forever. Being in his arms
once more was as close to heaven as Esther felt she'd
ever get.

Their kiss was long and passionate and in full view
of several hundred people. Carried away by their love,
they came back to earth with a jolt as Adair's voice
broke into their world.

"Before we hand her over to the good doctor for the
rest of the night, maybe we can talk Esther into working with me on this next tune. What do you say,
everybody?"

The old walls of the Great Hall seemed to reverberate
with the encouragement of the crowd. Esther looked
around at the sea of faces. She smiled her gratitude
and satisfaction and raised her hand in acknowledge-
ment.

From on top of the world she met Dan's gaze. She
saw the pride and love and joy he was feeling and knew
they were reflected in her own expression.

Over the roar Adair spoke out once more.

"What do you say, Doc? Can we borrow her for a few
minutes?"

"A very few minutes," Dan told Esther, who was the
only one close enough to hear him even though he was
shouting.

His next kiss was like a quick test to make sure she
was really there. Then he kissed her again for the sheer
pleasure of it and released her.

He watched as she moved toward the platform. Her

long gown silhouetting her tall, slim figure swayed seductively as she mounted the steps to center stage. Esther was beaming with happiness. Dan had never seen her look more beautiful.

"Oh, honey, I'm so happy for you," Adair said into Esther's ear as the two women embraced.

"Adair. Thank you. For everything," Esther said, meeting her friend's gaze before turning to face her loyal fans.

She allowed the reverence to continue for several more seconds, taking it in and holding it close to her heart. Her glance fell to Dan, who clapped and grinned as enthusiastically as her most devout follower.

"Thank you," she called out, leaning into Adair's microphone. "Thank you. It's great to be back."

As the din flared up once again, Esther moved to the piano, which has been set off toward stage right. Situated so that she could watch the crowd—and Dan— Esther took her place. She looked at Adair for her cue to start.

Esther began the mellifluous tune alone, but was soon joined by a section of strings that sweetened and romanticized the melody. Soon Adair's crystal-clear voice pealed out, making every word sound true and heartfelt.

> You were the one who took time to love me.
> You were the one who knew what love should be.
> You were the one who made my life worthwhile.
> Let me cry and made me smile.
> You were the one who believed in me.
> You are the only one for me.
>
> We made love, the way lovers do.
> Then you had to leave me.
> But don't you go too far away,
> It won't be long, believe me.
> I'll win you back and that's a fact.
> One that you can count on.

You belong to me, you're not free.
Our hearts are tied by destiny.

You were the one . . .

Esther played through the chorus automatically as
she looked over at Dan. He seemed to be in total awe,
as if watching a dream come true. Esther's heart swelled
to bursting, knowing his love, feeling his admiration,
aware that this man meant more to her than anything
else in the world.

No guarantees, no promises, no solemn vows.
No set of facts, no reasons why, no contract needed.
I am yours. You are mine.
Our lives are bound through endless time.
We fell in love, the way lovers do,
But don't think I'm through with you.
We've dreams to see, for you and me.
They're already coming true.

You were the one who took time to love me.
You were the one . . .

The song came to an end. The beautiful tribute to
Esther's love for Dan filled the still air for several seconds before the thunderous response from the audience began.

With Adair's help, Esther waved herself offstage, and
even though the throng called her back, she felt she'd
given them enough time. The rest of this night belonged to her and Dan alone.

As prearranged with Fesstus, Dan would meet her
backstage in Adair's dressing room. Normally a person
who took pride in her levelheadedness, Esther wasn't
at all embarrassed to find that her feet weren't even
touching the floor. She giggled irrepressibly in her excitement. Had she ever, in her entire life, been this

happy before? She didn't think so. And yet, sobering words from her last conversation with Addy came to mind.

Don't let him get away from you, young lady. Letting him go would be the biggest mistake you made since your last big mistake, Addy had said sternly.

Which mistake was that? I've made quite a few, you know, Esther had replied.

Letting go of me.

Esther smiled. She wasn't going to let go of anyone ever again. Addy had been the only good and loving person in her life as a child, and she'd turned her back on her because she was part of a past she wanted to forget.

She was much wiser now. She knew what a precious gift love was and how hard loyalty was to come by. Esther should have cherished Addy's love and faithfulness and returned it a hundredfold. Love wasn't something you turned your back on. It was something to be gathered up and held tightly. It was something to be given away freely. For it was in the giving and taking of love that life found its meaning.

Esther was loved . . . by Addy, her friends, and best of all by Dan. She knew how to love too. It was risky, she knew, but the rewards were worth the risks. The joy and happiness, and yes, the heartache and pain of the past few months, had made her feel more alive than she'd ever felt before. She was going to live the rest of her life out in knowing the happiness, the delight, and, if necessary, the sorrow of loving those closest to her. Never again would she hide her heart away from those who loved her or those who needed her to love them.

Esther turned as she heard the door opening. Dan stood in the doorway, tall and handsome and real . . . and grinning from ear to ear.

"Hi," he said.

"Hi," Esther said. She suddenly felt nervous and awkward, torn between throwing herself into his arms and waiting to see what he was going to do.

"People say you're a genius, and if anyone were to ask me, I'd have to say it was true."

Esther laughed, recalling their first coherent conversation the morning after her fever broke, so many months ago.

"You've certainly changed *your* tune, Doctor. I suppose the next thing you'll be saying is how crazy in love with me you are."

"Actually all that stuff was third on my list," Dan said, stepping into the room and closing the door behind him.

Esther frowned in curiosity. Her heart was hammering, her nerve endings jumping with excitement. The last thing she wanted to do was talk. "Hello, I love you," was all she'd wanted to hear.

"What was the second thing you were going to say?" she finally had to ask.

Dan's eyes were dancing with merriment, his smile teasing as he stretched out his hands and said, "What the hell took you so long?"

His welcoming, outstretched arms, the tender, loving expression on his face, were all Esther needed. In one motion she moved into his embrace and pressed her lips to his in a long overdue, well-deserved kiss. It was a joining of the bodies, hearts, and spirit of two people who had fought hard to reach that moment. This time it would be forever. This time there wasn't a doubt in her mind, or an insecurity in her heart to cloud her love. This time she gave to him a whole, complete woman. A woman who believed in herself, in him, and in their future together.

Epilogue

Excerpts from a young's girl's diary:

"Today in gym class Ellen told me Geoff Walston likes me. I saved a seat at the asembly for him, but he didn't sit in it.

"Got the job on the school paper. Now all I need is a really great story.

"Daddy took us to the Grammy's in New York last weekend. He said the hospital could run itself for a few days. Mom got another award. We went to see Uncle Eddy, who is really our cousin, but we call him uncle because he's old. He showed us pictures of the building he blew up so he could build his new one where the old one was. Mark and Jason thought it was pretty great. I liked playing with his new baby. Her name is Heather.

"Daddy decided to drive us home instead of flying. It took forever. We went through this old place that had a mine in it. Mom said when she was thirteen, like me, she lived there. She laughed when we went into this weird store to get drinks. She said they still haven't changed the signs. Daddy laughed, too, so I think it was probably one of their old jokes. We didn't spend the night there. We stayed in a hotel in Maryland. I was glad to leave. I can't imagine what Mom did there for fun.

"I want to get my hair cut. No one else I know has hair as long as mine. Mom says she can't cut it, it's too beautiful. Daddy says if I lived in a convent, I could wear it as short as I like. I think he was joking.

"Gramma Addy died today. Mom cried. I'm going to miss her too. We're all going to Bellewood for the funeral. I don't know why we have to bury her there, but Mom says it's what Gramma Addy wanted. I really am going to miss her. She said Mom did some pretty crazy things when she was sixteen and that if I want my hair short, I should just get it cut.

"Spent the night at Clare's. Mom says Tony Westlake called last night while I was gone. Dad went on and on about the convent again. Mom just laughed.

"Found this in my history book this morning.

> I try to tell you every day
> In every sort of way,
> You're the daughter that I dreamed of
> And you'll always have my love.
>
> Mom

"I love you, too, Mom.

"I may have to kill Mark and Jason. I tell people I don't know who they are, and just about the time I have everyone convinced, one of them will come up and ask for money or give me a message from Mom.

"She didn't say much when she saw my haircut. She just smiled and said it was very pretty, that I should have had it cut long ago. Later she told me Daddy almost cried.

"Mom said I'm a very lucky girl and I should be

grateful for all I have. I pretty much am for the most part. I think I'd be happier as an only child, though. Daddy says I'll appreciate Mark and Jason when we're all older, but I seriously doubt it.

THE EDITOR'S CORNER

Have you been having fun with our **HOMETOWN HUNK CONTEST**? If not, hurry and join in the excitement by entering a gorgeous local man to be a LOVESWEPT cover hero. The deadline for entries is September 15, 1988, and contest rules are in the back of our books. Now, if you need some inspiration, we have six incredible hunks in our LOVESWEPTs this month . . . and you can dream about the six to come next month . . . to get you in the mood to discover one of your own.

First next month, there's Jake Kramer, "danger in the flesh," the fire fighter hero of new author Terry Lawrence's **WHERE THERE'S SMOKE, THERE'S FIRE,** LOVESWEPT #288. When Jennie Cisco sets eyes on Jake, she knows she's in deep trouble—not so much because of the fire he warns her is racing out of control toward her California retreat, as because of the man himself. He is one tough, yet tender, and decidedly sexy man . . . and Jennie isn't the least bit prepared for his steady and potent assault on her senses and her soul. A musician who can no longer perform, Jenny has secluded herself in the mountains. She fiercely resists Jake's advances . . . until she learns that it may be more terrifying to risk losing him than to risk loving him. A romance that blazes with passion!

Our next hunk-of-the-month, pediatrician Patrick Hunter, will make you laugh along with heroine Megan Murphy as he irresistibly attracts her in **THANKSGIVING,** LOVESWEPT #289, by Janet Evanovich. In this absolutely delightful romance set in Williamsburg, Virginia, at turkey time, Megan and Dr. Pat suddenly find themselves thrown together as the temporary parents of an abandoned baby. Wildly attracted to each

(continued)

other, both yearn to turn their "playing house" into the real thing, yet circumstances *and* Megan's past conspire to keep them apart . . . until she learns that only the doctor who kissed her breathless can heal her lonely heart. A love story as full of chuckles as it is replete with the thrills of falling in love.

Move over Crocodile Dundee, because we've got an Aussie hero to knock the socks off any woman! Brig McKay is a hell-raiser, to be sure, and one of the most devastatingly handsome men ever to cross the path of Deputy Sheriff Millie Surprise, in LOVESWEPT #290, **CAUGHT BY SURPRISE,** by Deborah Smith. Brig has to do some time in Millie's jail, and after getting to know the petite and feisty officer, he's determined to make it a life sentence! But in the past Millie proved to be too much for the men in her life to take, and she's sure she'll turn out to be an embarrassment to Brig. You'll delight in the rollicking, exciting, merry chase as Brig sets out to capture his lady for all time. A delight!

You met that good-looking devil Jared Loring this month, and next Joan Elliott Pickart gives you his own beguiling love story in **MAN OF THE NIGHT,** LOVESWEPT #291. Tabor O'Casey needed Jared's help to rescue her brother, who'd vanished on a mysterious mission, and so she'd called on this complicated and enigmatic man who'd befriended her father. Jared discovers he can refuse her nothing. Though falling as hard and fast for Tabor as she is falling for him, Jared suspects her feelings. And, even in the midst of desperate danger, Tabor must pit herself against the shadowed soul of this man and dare to prove him wrong about her love. A breathlessly beautiful romance!

Here is inspirational hunk #5: Stone Hamilton, one glorious green-eyed, broad-shouldered man and the hero of **TIME OUT,** LOVESWEPT #292, by Patt

(continued)

Bucheister. Never have two people been so mismatched as Stone and beautiful Whitney Grant. He's an efficiency expert; she doesn't even own a watch. He's supremely well-organized, call him Mr. Order; she's delightfully scattered, call her Miss Creativity. Each knows that something *has* to give as they are drawn inexorably into a love affair as hot as it is undeniable. Just how these two charming opposites come to resolve their conflicts will make for marvelous reading next month.

Would you believe charismatic, brawny, handsome, *and* rich? Well, that's just what hero Sam Garrett is! You'll relish his all-out efforts to capture the beautiful and winsome Max Strahan, in **WATER WITCH,** LOVESWEPT #293, by Jan Hudson. Hired to find water on a rocky Texas ranch, geologist Max doesn't want anyone to know her methods have nothing to do with science—and everything to do with the mystical talent of using a dowsing stick. Sam's totally pragmatic—except when it comes to loving Max, whose pride and independence are at war with her reckless desire for the man she fears will laugh at her "gift." Then magic, hot and sweet, takes over and sets this glorious romance to simmering! A must-read love story.

Enjoy all the hunks this month and every month!

Carolyn Nichols

Carolyn Nichols
  Editor
LOVESWEPT
Bantam Books
666 Fifth Avenue
New York, NY 10103

THE DELANEY DYNASTY

Men and women whose loves and passions are so glorious it takes many great romance novels by three bestselling authors to tell their tempestuous stories.

THE SHAMROCK TRINITY

THE DELANEYS OF KILLAROO

Now Available!
THE DELANEYS: *The Untamed Years*

NEW!

Handsome Book Covers Specially Designed To Fit Loveswept Books

Our new French Calf Vinyl book covers come in a set of three great colors—royal blue, scarlet red and kachina green.

Each 7" × 9½" book cover has two deep vertical pockets, a handy sewn-in bookmark, and is soil and scratch resistant.

To order your set, use the form below.

Special Offer
Buy a Bantam Book
for only 50¢.

Now you can have Bantam's catalog filled with hundreds of titles plus take advantage of our unique and exciting bonus book offer. A special offer which gives you the opportunity to purchase a Bantam book for only 50¢. Here's how!

By ordering any five books at the regular price per order, you can also choose any other single book listed (up to a $5.95 value) for just 50¢. Some restrictions do apply, but for further details why not send for Bantam's catalog of titles today!

Just send us your name and address and we will send you a catalog!
